BEHIND THE

To my sister, Maggie

Behind the Sofa

ANTHONY THACKER

KINGSWAY PUBLICATIONS
EASTBOURNE

Contents

Introduction   7

1. Behind the Sofa   11
2. The Doctor's Companion   25
3. The Evil of the Universe   35
4. Who Is the Doctor?   43
5. The Occult Universe of Doctor Who   55
6. Doctor Who After 9/11   67
7. The Evil of the Daleks   79
8. Manipulating Myth Makers   89
9. Time Travelling Temptations   99
10. The Doctor in the Moral Maze   111
11. Sex in the TARDIS   127
12. Horror, Fangs and Suspense   135
13. The Living TARDIS   141
14. Blasphemers Will Be Exterminated!   153
15. Return of the Cybermen   159

Epilogue   171

Introduction

Dead and gone

They said it would never return: 'Time is, time was, time is past.'[1] And *Doctor Who* was history. But the Time Traveller has a funny habit of breaking the laws of time. Twice before, the programme recovered from execution, returning in 1986 after an 18-month pause and in the 1996 film after a seven-year wait. Then it was firmly laid to rest. RIP.

But here it is again. The corpse won't stay dead; it is more alive than ever.

However, the twenty-first century is no longer fiction. We live in it. What does *Doctor Who* have to say to a century reshaped by 9/11? With its moral certainties about evil, what could it offer a postmodern age that trades in moral complexity? And how could the Doctor and his ever-present (if changing) companion fit in today's world of the Internet, conspiracy theories and WMD – an age where the race to map the genome has overtaken the space race in the popular imagination?

---

[1] Caption to the cartoon from the title page of Elizabeth Allde's 1630 edition of Robert Greene's *The Honorable Historie of Frier Bacon and Frier Bongay*.

Would it be able to handle the changing religious climate, where 'religious hatred' is not a history lesson but triggers today's government bills?

We now know the answers, some of them anyway. And with its greater depth of characterisation, *Doctor Who* offers itself more than ever as a launch pad for discussion on the social, moral and religious issues of the day between parents and children, youth leaders and the teenagers or pre-teens in their groups, and indeed for those adults who also form part of its large audience. And this book opens up these discussions.

Some ask whether the new series is old *Doctor Who* stories redone. And similarly, some may fear this book is just the *Doctor Who* sections of my earlier book, *A Closer Look at Science Fiction*, repackaged, or worse, repeated, but with one extra chapter added. I will spare you that frustration! This *will* be a fresh close look at the world of *Doctor Who*. Although I make connections with earlier stories, it is centred on the new series and not just updated with new examples. It opens up new angles, as the new series pitches some of the traditional themes in a very different way, and it also raises new issues. But one thing won't change: I still think *Doctor Who* presents good, popular science fiction for a wide audience, and that it not only provokes the imagination (of various possible futures, for example), but also provides a revealing mirror to the challenges of life as we experience them right now.

Doctor Who works because it is an adventure series which has at its heart the possibility of the Doctor and his companion(s) finding themselves in any imaginable situations in any context in time and space, and even beyond them. Good writers can be challenged by the vast possibilities of fresh angles this provides.

Will the real *Doctor Who* please stand up?

Some fans of the old show may question if this is real *Doctor Who*! It's a bit like the debate among *Star Trek* fans, where some prefer the original series with Captain Kirk and his famous half-Vulcan Science Officer, Mr Spock, while others say that *Star Trek: The Next Generation* (and its successors) with Captain Picard, Data and the rest provides the mature product. I'm sure this *Doctor Who* debate will also continue. For clarity, I will distinguish between them, mostly talking of the series from 1963 to 1996 as 'classic' *Doctor Who*, and the current programme as 'new' *Doctor Who*. If I talk simply of *Doctor Who*, then I will mean the whole series, classic and current.

One element is common to both *Star Trek* and *Doctor Who*: the later *Star Trek* concentrated on deeper characterisation, unlike the original series, in which we know precious little even about characters as central as Scottie. And the biggest difference in new *Doctor Who* (apart from the sad loss of that iconic element of classic *Doctor Who*, the cliff-hanger) is the stronger, deeper, more consistent and credible characterisation.

As for the missing cliff-hanger, it's worth noting, for fans of the classic series who are looking for new *Doctor Who* much more in the classic style, that there are now over 70 audio stories in the *Big Finish* series, with 25-minute episodes, complete with cliff-hangers. What's more, they star the Fifth, Sixth,

Seventh and Eighth Doctors (as played by Peter Davison, Colin Baker, Sylvester McCoy and Paul McGann), plus relevant companions, and include stories every bit as good as the best of the original series. The series is also prepared to take on challenging issues. One example is religious themes, which go beyond the classic stereotype of human-sacrifice cliff-hanger. For example, one of the most recent stories places the Fifth Doctor in *The Council of Nicaea*, that momentous occasion in the fourth century when Christian theologians shaped up the foundations of Christian teaching as expressed in our creeds. Fancy hearing the Doctor quoting Romans 16? Or wonder what it would be like if the Doctor met the Emperor Constantine, and the battling theologians Athanasius and Arius – and somehow got his headstrong female companions into the Council itself?

Finally, I write in a way that is of course true to my own perspective as a fan who is also a Christian (and indeed a Baptist minister). But I also trust that readers who are not Christians will find that this book gives them a different matrix to explore the show.

Of my first, far more broadly based book, Vanessa Bishop in *Doctor Who Magazine* commented, 'Thacker never writes his SF-tinted theology so deeply you lose him, and it's always interesting to see familiar material in different arenas.'[2] I hope you will find this true of *Behind the Sofa*.

---

[2] Vanessa Bishop: review of Anthony Thacker: *A Closer Look at Science Fiction* in *Doctor Who Magazine #309* (17 October 2001).

1

Behind the Sofa

Back in the TARDIS

Doctor Who is not just back; it's back big time. It has far exceeded BBC expectations. The 'regeneration', not simply of the Ninth Doctor, but of the series, works very well in terms of viewing figures.

After years of serving up repeats of episodes, which fans had seen many times, to dwindling audiences, the BBC was surprised by the phenomenal success of genuinely new *Doctor Who*. Nearly eleven million watched the first episode; this not only makes it comparable with all but a handful of the most viewed episodes of the old show ever, but it does so in the new era of scores of TV channels and was beaten only by a small number of soap episodes that week.

Even after the initial interest and curiosity of the first episode died down, each episode since has gathered around seven to nine million viewers. *Doctor Who* has repeatedly made it to the front pages of the tabloids, as the developments of the show represent big news. Science fiction and

TV magazines compete with each other for their coverage of *Doctor Who* as the biggest thing by far in the genre, right now – all this and the awards for top actor (Christopher Eccleston), top actress (Billie Piper) and top drama on British television (for *Doctor Who* itself) in the October 2005 National Television Awards (the British TV equivalent of the Oscars). So the series is back for season two and even season three in 2007.

The BBC should not have been surprised. Similar figures were achieved for the 1996 film (nearly nine million in the UK, as well as similar figures in the States, although that represented too small a share of the US viewing figures for that US-based project to be taken further).

But this new series is attracting far more viewers than classic *Doctor Who* did in its last few years. Bearing in mind the lower viewing figures for any one channel generally today, these compare well with the most successful phases of the show.

What is the basis for the new *Doctor Who*'s success? I'm sure the original and traditional teatime Saturday slot is a factor. Certainly no giant mistake has been made, like pitching it against *Coronation Street* (as was tried in the 1980s).

But a large part of its success is down to the basic formula, much of which has not changed, together with strong casting and well-written plots. Most importantly, the show successfully operates at several different levels, as we will see. These ensure that the show appeals to children of different ages, as well as to many teenagers and adults. It is, unusually, a TV show for all the family, and so there is tremendous potential for parents in this. Christian parents, and indeed all parents keen to foster good, positive relations across their family as a whole, can find something positive in this appeal.

Now some may react only to the challenges they feel, because of the questions of fear, violence, and its perspective on sexual morality. But others will recognise instead a great opportunity. For once, in our fragmented culture, something will be recognised and understood by a large number of children, teenagers and adults alike, and a common language can be used to talk about some important issues of life. Many in youth and children's work will want to take advantage of the opportunities this offers to them.

The new series contains many parallels with classic *Doctor Who*, and some episodes are either very like classic stories (compare *Rose* with *Spearhead from Space*), or at least contain some interesting similarities (see *Dalek* and *Power of the Daleks*). But then that was true of the original series, too: the first episode and a half of *Castrovalva* is reminiscent in some key ways of *The Edge of Destruction*; and Terry Nation was quite happy to redo whole sequences in *Planet of the Daleks*, plagiarised from his own earlier Dalek stories (invisible aliens, hiding inside a Dalek, throwing heavy weights onto the Dalek pursuing the heroes up a lift-shaft, etc.).

But the new series has genuinely new ideas, too. However, what makes it really different, as will become clear, is the depth of characterisation.

We have already seen how *Doctor Who* – certainly when firing on all cylinders – works in a multi-layered way. For teens and adults there is good characterisation and plot development, and for children – scary monsters!

Big Bad Wolf

The 'bad wolf' theme shaped the first season of this new *Doctor Who* series, starting with the merest hints, as in *The Unquiet Dead* (where Victorian maid Gwyneth talks in a natural enough metaphorical way of the 'big bad wolf'), but concluding the season with an overall plot resolution. But as we settle down on (or behind) the sofa, the image is a useful starter. For the 'big bad wolf', the monster of fairy tales, is centre stage in *Doctor Who*, both classic and current. And from the beginning it has been a debating point between some parents and their children. The Cybermen were among the most scary of the original monsters, including (as we shall see) for the young Russell T. Davies. And after their vintage performance in *The Tomb of the Cybermen* (1967), the feedback programme *Talkback*, anchored by David Coleman, featured the issue of whether *Doctor Who* and its Cybermen were just too scary to be allowed on TV during the early evening. '. . . *Doctor Who:* Is it too violent for the children? Or perhaps it really came back to: Is it too violent for the parents?' mused Coleman.

Horror, violence, blasphemy, sex and the occult

So, is *Doctor Who* dangerous, with all its horror and violence? For Christians, there's also the question of religion, the occult – and additional issues in this new series about Daleks and blasphemy, not to mention the very different way it handles questions of sex and relationships.

If frightened children 'hide behind the sofa', to what extent is it sensible to subject children to a show with this degree of horror? There is also the issue of the moral perspective of the show, which is not identical to that held by many Christians. And some parents struggle with the whole area of fantasy and imagination, recognising the possibilities that it can mislead as well as help.

You will be exterminated!

What's it like to meet a Dalek? A real one? No, not for the Doctor and his companions. But for you? And what if you were only five, or even three? Facetious question? Not for my five-year-old and three-year-old, some fourteen years ago.

It was a very wet day, and I had taken my two older boys, Chris and Alex (or Sandy, as we called him then), on a rainy expedition to a local bookshop in Leicester, where leading *Doctor Who* novelist Terence Dicks was signing his books for sale. But there was an added attraction – a real, full-sized Dalek would be there.

The shop was very crowded. What was going on further in the shop – the queue for book signing and the rest – was well hidden. But suddenly, as we moved through the crowd, there it was: a Dalek! Chris (aged five) flinched. After all, it was not some model; it was moving! He gripped my hand tightly, though Sandy (aged three) took it in his stride. However, as Dad seemed not to be worried, Chris eased off for a few moments, as we got nearer – until the next thing happened. A shopper photographed the Dalek with flash. The Dalek glided towards her, moving its eye-stick in her direction, and then spoke, with its familiar grating voice: 'If – you – do – that – again – you – will – be – exterminated!' The giggles of the shoppers did not allay Chris's concern. There was no sofa to hide behind – but hiding behind Dad was definitely in order.

However, as Dad said it was alright, he relaxed again, and we passed the Dalek and joined the queue for the book-signing. All this time, while Chris was still giving the Dalek wary looks, Sandy carried on without a worry. That was not because he was ignorant of Daleks. He had by this time seen several episodes of *Doctor Who*, as the BBC had taken to scheduling repeats straight after their repeats of *Thunderbirds*, which was already a firm favourite. He had seen the Daleks, and knew what they could do on television. But as his Dad seemed not to be worried, neither was he.

Meanwhile, the Dalek moved towards us, and started addressing one or two individuals here and there in the queue. Then it approached Sandy, and prodded him with its plunger: 'Who – are – you? What – is – your – name?' 'Sandy,' replied the three-year-old, this time with a quiver in his voice (quickly consoled by Dad!).

I mention this episode as it shows that even at three, although a child has not fully separated off fantasy and reality, it is clear that he could recognise the difference between the television situation and the reality in a Leicester shop. But it also illustrates some of the difficulties for the younger child. Both children had a genuine element of fear that no adult would have experienced in the same circumstances – and both children overcame their fears. On this subject, Russell

T. Davies comments: 'There's not a child on the planet who watches *Finding Nemo* and thinks that's a real fish.'[1] But he recognises the fear will be real, and cites his own experience back in the 1970s of 'nightmares of Cybermen'. But his aim is to have more monsters, not fewer, and says, 'Bring on those nightmares!' Incidentally, Alex tells me now that if it had been a Cyberman in that shop, then he really would have been afraid!

How should a parent of younger children feel, or act? And what if you think your child will have nightmares?

It's the monsters, stupid!

What is the attraction of *Doctor Who?* When it comes to younger children, it's the monsters every time! Stephen, my youngest, is not exactly young, now, but as a Down's syndrome child, he shares this passion for the monster stories, preferring especially stories with Cybermen and Ice Warriors. And while he will now opt for a story where obvious monsters are less prominent, like *The Two Doctors*, I take that as a sign of his beginning to grow beyond that 'younger child' set of interests.

For the younger child, you can forget the details of character, or even plot. For them: It's the monsters, stupid (to adapt Bill Clinton's election slogan)!

Who – or what – are these monsters? And what do they represent? Monsters, of course, abound in many children's fairy

---

[1] Russell T. Davies, as told to Christopher Middleton, in *Radio Times: Doctor Who Special* (2005), p. 2.

tales. Some are exaggerations of everyday realities – fear of the dark, of spiders, of the unknown. What would it be like to face a spider or insects as large as we are and as clever? Some *Doctor Who* stories, like *The Web Planet* and *Planet of the Spiders*, have answered that.

Other monsters are not only frightening in themselves, but they also represent the awful thought that the human race could go terribly wrong, that we could turn *ourselves* into monsters. Daleks and Cybermen express that double threat.

Other monsters represent the idea that there are evil powers in the universe, powers that do not wish us well, powers that would like to take over our minds, our lives, our world, and destroy any who resist. When we think of the evils unleashed by the régimes of Adolf Hitler, Pol Pot and others, we realise that this form of evil does not exist only as a fantasy of the imagination; unfortunately, it can be all too real. For Christians, there is another powerful resonance here. Evil is real, and for the Christian, there is a spiritual dimension to the need to resist evil.

Science fiction pictures this in terms of alien attack. Powers like the Nestene Consciousness, at work through Autons, or indeed the Slitheen, illustrate this attempt to take over the world. Obviously, the stories in themselves illustrate a gigantic 'What if?' What if there really were hostile aliens who tried to take over and destroy us? The basic answer of *Doctor Who* to this question functions as a picture of resisting evil – and of finding a 'Saviour' to help us. At least, that was true of classic *Doctor Who*. It is a curious feature of the first season of the new series that the Doctor only saves the day once, in the climactic threat of the ten stories – in *The End of the World*.[2] Elsewhere, the decisive action was mostly taken by Rose or the TARDIS, or occasionally by others, like her boyfriend, Mickey, and her dad, Pete. We will have to see if seasons two and three continue this deconstruction of the Doctor's historic rôle.

Now there is another underlying element: the aliens can be an allegory (deliberate or accidental) of humans who behave in a way that is alien to what humans should be. What if some humans behave like the monsters? Maybe the attitude to monsters can represent the response to fear, and also illustrate ways in which it is right to react to the many forms evil can take.

But some may think that if the programme could trigger nightmares, and could be too disturbing, why should parents even *think* of letting their young children watch it?

Not all children are alike, so each parent should take the time necessary to judge the impact of *Doctor Who* – like everything else – on their children. Some children scare more easily; some will have very vivid, recurring nightmares, and very disturbed sleep (for children and parents!), while others won't.

However, I'm going to assume that at least one parent will

---

[2] To save 'nitpickers guide' uncertainty, let me say that, as I see it, in the final crisis of each story the threat is resolved (in order) by: Rose; the Doctor; Gwyneth; Mickey; Rose/the Dalek; Cathica; Pete; Nancy; the TARDIS; the TARDIS/Rose. It is of course true that the Doctor sometimes played a rôle, guiding Mickey and Nancy, for example, and that he saved people on other occasions, e.g., in the cliff-hanger resolution at the start of *The Doctor Dances*.

be with the children during the programme, and that they are not having an extreme response, but something of a normal level of fear, which the parents may have had if *they* watched the programme in their childhood. If the child is too upset or frightened, there's no benefit in them watching. But what if they need a parent there, to dare to watch it? I think there's a great advantage for parents spending time with their children in this way, as we shall see.

Monsters are an enormous part of the world of *Doctor Who*; however, as we have seen, they vary, as do the threats and challenges they represent. So, in many chapters of this book, we will return to the monsters. As we look at the stories of the new series, and illustrate the issues they also raise from many earlier stories, we will explore what this means in our twenty-first-century world.

Evil must be fought

There is a consistent moral dimension to *Doctor Who*. The Doctor is pictured as a hero. He is not, generally, indifferent to the problems he faces, but consistently determined to face them in a moral way. Russell T. Davies, the mastermind of the new series is in agreement with this: the Doctor 'makes people better'. This is not as a conventional doctor does, of course! He makes people better morally, not physically. This is explored very strongly in Rose's growing moral commitment in the series, and the difficulties for her boyfriend and mother in keeping up with her new development of moral purpose.

This has long been a factor in *Doctor Who*. The Second Doctor, in the 1967 story *The Moonbase*, put it this way:

'There are some corners of the universe which have bred the most terrible things – things which act against everything we believe in. They must be fought.'

The Second Doctor, in *The Moonbase*

But the new series has pressed things in a new way, and will raise new questions for those watching the series. The polarities have not been reversed – but they have been realigned! This can and should make for some very creative and positive discussions ahead. For the 9–14-year-old that *Doctor Who* has been designed to attract, a vital part is the sense of adventure. Some mysteries, some puzzles should be thrown up here. Where *has* the Doctor landed? What on earth is really going on? As one who first watched the programme in that age group, I found that element very important at the time.

But another thing that is clear about the over-nines group is that this is an age when moral consciousness is becoming strongly established. A nine-year-old more than a six-year-old understands deliberate intent, and has a sense of signing up to what he or she thinks is right. The highly moral character of *Doctor Who*, with its central theme of the struggle against evil, works very well with that. The earliest *Doctor Who* stories engaged with both of these dimensions straight away. The first episode of 1963, *An Unearthly Child*, was full of mystery – who was this strange person and her even stranger grandfather? And *what* was going to happen to them? *100,000 BC* placed these awkwardly displaced unwilling partners in the most primitive human context ever attempted. Would they abuse their powers? Would they succumb to becoming primitive themselves, like an adult version of *Lord of the Flies?* And the story which followed, *The Daleks*, was full of moral questions about deceit and truth, nuclear war and pacifism, tolerance and racial hatred, as well as a pioneering sequence of adventures.

What *Doctor Who* presents for the older child and parent together is a context for dealing with such moral questions. The new series of *Doctor Who*, as we shall see, is not afraid of repitching this moral dimension in a twenty-first-century world that is much more at home with single-parent families and questions of homosexual as well as heterosexual attraction than the world of 1963.

Doctor Who's Who

For the older teenager, and for adults of course, character is very important. This was an area of frequent weakness in the original series, which Russell T. Davies has sought to correct. The series stands or falls with the character of the Doctor, of course. Present a weak characterisation, and the series will be fatally flawed. But the next most important characters are the companions. There, the original series too often started with a strong character, but allowed characterisation of this supposed intellectual heavyweight or Rambo to drift into the rôle of screamer.

Russell T. Davies has rightly fought hard to correct that, as we shall see when we look at the Doctor's companion (Chapter 2). A different danger beckons. The contemporary need to have fast-paced stories can undercut the need to spend time in the development of characters particular to a story. Even more so, it takes away some of the build-up of tension and suspense. However, we will find that this provides plenty of context to look at how people change and grow – and what sorts of experiences help with such changes. So there is plenty of material here for teens and those who work with them. As we look at the stories, we will not only examine the great challenges and moral issues, but also those arising out of characterisation.

2

The Doctor's Companion

To enter the world of *Doctor Who* is to be confronted by dangers often of an extraordinary kind. What would it be like for you or me to enter that TARDIS and, through its gateway, enter the Doctor's experience? In effect, you and I *are* the companion. Rose Tyler is an ordinary person caught up in the world of the Doctor. First off, she is suddenly amidst the threat of the 'Nestene Consciousness', a vat of living plastic in control of armed plastic mannequins, and much more follows. Her world, and in another way that of her mother, Jackie, and boyfriend, Mickey, is turned upside down. Yet Rose is no mere spectator. This is twenty-first-century *Doctor Who*, and from the Nestene Consciousness to the Daleks, Rose saves the Doctor – not the other way round.

Why the companion?

In the 26 years of *Doctor Who* from 1963 to 1989, with over 150 stories, in only one story did the Doctor appear without a companion (*The Deadly Assassin*). Indeed, the presence of companions – and their turnover – is such a constant that the last of these, Ace, when quizzed by recurring star Brigadier Lethbridge-Stewart, retorts witheringly, 'Just call me "the latest one"!' (*Battlefield* – untransmitted sequence, shown in the video *More Than Thirty Years in the TARDIS*.)

The character of the companion is central to *Doctor Who* – and is therefore central to the comparative success or failure of any phase of the show. A Christian might think of Jesus and his disciples, whom he calls 'friends' (John 15:13–15), for in a way, the companion is a disciple – and Rose is a particularly fast learner. If we look at some of the previous companions, we can see examples of great strength, but also of mistakes and failures.

In this context, Rose Tyler is a first. She is the first and only companion to last longer in *Doctor Who* than her Doctor. That does not yet make her anything like the longest lasting companion, as of course Christopher Eccleston was (with the exception of the Eighth Doctor) the shortest running Doctor, in terms of both number of episodes and time in the rôle. Jamie McCrimmon was the Doctor's longest serving companion, involved in every story of the Second Doctor except the very first, and was in *Doctor Who* for three years, from 1966 to 1969, and several other companions stayed with the series for two years.

But as we shall see, the way the story of Rose is drawn makes her rôle quite different from those who came before her, though some features are very much in continuity with what went before.

So who are the companions?

Not counting UNIT soldiers, 28 people accompanied the Doctor in his adventures until Doctor Grace Holloway joined him in the 1996 film, and now Rose (and of course Jack Harkness).

There have been many variations, including the number of companions. The series began with the elderly First Doctor and his granddaughter, Susan, who, by a series of mistakes, are joined, reluctantly, by two of Susan's human school-teachers, Ian and Barbara. The early stories are characterised by sequences of dramatic conflict in an atmosphere reflective of the 'angry young men' of John Osborne (of *Look Back in Anger* fame) and others. As often happened with *Doctor Who*, however, the needs of the next adventure softened the hard edges of conflict, or indeed personality, as we shall see.

Question: In the over 160 stories of *Doctor Who*, which is the more common pattern: the Doctor with only one companion, or with more than one? Answer to come later! While you carry on thinking, we'll look at the evidence.

The First Doctor is accompanied by two or three companions in every story except *The Massacre*, where (if we ignore the interlude after the story is over, and the Doctor 'accidentally' picks up Dodo Chaplet) only Stephen Taylor accompanies the Doctor. The Second Doctor not only has Jamie in every story except the first, but also Ben and Polly in the first two stories, and later Victoria, and finally Zoe.

The Third Doctor has one female companion (Liz, then Jo,

then Sarah), though his stories often also feature the Brigadier and the Team at UNIT. This pattern (with Harry Sullivan as the UNIT man) continued for the first few Fourth Doctor stories. But for most of his seven years, if we discount K-9, he was with just one companion: Sarah, then Leela, then Romana (in two regenerations).

By the end of the Fourth Doctor, and through much of the Fifth Doctor, this pattern of having three or four companions was repeated, but to my mind without the success of the original quartet. The conflicts between the companions and with the Doctor tried but failed to recreate the tensions between Ian and the First Doctor (despite some good acting, especially from Janet Fielding's Tegan Jovanka), and was an unsatisfactory dimension of what was otherwise a very strong sequence of stories. The clarity of Peri, by contrast, showed a better form. This is even more clearly shown in more recent audio adventures, where the Fifth Doctor appears with just Nyssa. And the same is true with Turlough, and I expect (now actress Janet Fielding has agreed) when Tegan reappears. And from this point on, until the Ninth Doctor, with the exception of overlap stories (*Dragonfire*), the norm had been to see the Doctor with one, female companion – though in *The Two Doctors*, the Second Doctor is accompanied just by Jamie.

However, what we see from this is that it's not the number of companions, but the way they're written for that counts – and of course whether they are played by good actors. To my mind, Nicholas Courtney showed how it should be done. He played Alastair Gordon Lethbridge-Stewart, the Brigadier of UNIT, in a considerable number of stories over the years, and was given some pretty mediocre lines from time to time.

However, as a professional, he managed to turn them into something believable each time.

That said, writing for the companions did not always succeed, as, notoriously, a string of strong heroines turned into mindless screamers. Vicki, a brilliant orphan, and Zoe, a brilliant astrophysicist, provide two clear examples. Quickly, scriptwriters forgot their strengths, and simply placed them in jeopardy, screaming.

So does the Doctor normally have just one companion or more? Well the answer is: It depends if you think of the Brigadier (and his UNIT friends), or indeed K-9, as companions. If either is, then the Doctor normally has more than one companion; if not, then just one, who is nearly always female.

Rose

Rose is the first episode actually to be named after a companion, though it is not the only one where the companion is so centre stage. The first new companion, after the departure of the Doctor's granddaughter, was Vicki, in *The Rescue* – a simple short story which includes a dramatic threat, but in which the character of the new companion is central. Indeed, the earliest drafts of this story (where she had first been named Tanni) were entitled *Doctor Who and Tanni*. Vicki was presented as an orphan, whose only companion was in fact (and unknown to her) the murderer of her parents, and from whom she was saved. The story thus explains why it would be necessary for the Doctor to rescue her and take her with him. But she also becomes a kind of substitute granddaughter, brilliant like Susan, but also in need of protection.

Rose is very different. She is very much an ordinary, contemporary person – someone the viewers can identify with – and in that sense is more like Barbara, or even more like Peri. Some *Doctor Who* traditionalists complain that she seems too 'common' for their taste, charging that the TARDIS has landed in 'chav city'. But Dodo and Ben were cockneys before her – though writers then drew back from the implications of this, particularly with Dodo in *The Ark*, where the accent of actress Jackie Lane notoriously was obliged to change from more cockney to nearer 'standard English'! But even if it could be argued that Rose starts off as a 'chav', she does not remain limited by the stereotypes of that subculture.

For there is a way in which the character of Rose is very different from all others before, and reveals one of the strongest changes in the new series compared with the old: the development of her character. The clearest aspect of this is the way we get to know her relationships and friendships. We see her mother and boyfriend clearly. The contrast with the classic series is very marked here. Very few companions' relatives appear. The Brigadier's wife does not appear until his last story, and we still know next to nothing about her. Victoria's father appears before she does – and is murdered by the Daleks. The Doctor commiserating with her loss two full episodes after the end of that story is a very unusual and touching exception in classic *Doctor Who*. Similarly, in the enchanting tale *The Keeper of Traken*, Nyssa's father was killed by the Master, who also murdered Tegan's aunt in the following story, *Logopolis*. So all these stories show no continuing family relationships after these companions join the Doctor.

The nearest we get to the development of friendships in the classic series was in the UNIT era of the Third Doctor, but the relationships of Lethbridge-Stewart, Benton, and Yates are stylised both by the military context and by the way the plot drives the characters. So if Yates develops an interest in Buddhism, it's largely because the plot needs it.

By contrast, the characters in the new series are pressed much more clearly. So even by the end of the first episode, we feel we're beginning to get to know pretty clearly what makes Rose's mother tick, for example. These interludes may feel almost like soaps at first. But as the context develops, we see something more: how an ordinary person like us could react to the extraordinary pressures Rose faces. It is in contrast with her boyfriend and her mother that we see the development and growth of Rose's personality. In addition, we see a successful handling of conflict, more realistic because the context is more natural and thought through than any since the original tense context of Ian Chesterton against the First Doctor, when there was a strong element of anger at being hurled into dangers unwillingly.

Another positive feature is how the new series has successfully managed to have a strong Doctor and strong companion, perhaps for the first time. Arguably, the Seventh Doctor and Ace achieved that. But perhaps the strength of that companion was achieved at the expense of the Doctor. Again, we go back to Ian for comparable strength of both companion and Doctor. And Rose's strength is unusual for *Doctor Who*, where strong (or originally strong) companions have usually either been brainboxes (Vicki, Zoe, Liz, Romana, Nyssa), or macho women (Leela, Ace). Rose is a comparatively strong example of an ordinary person, and matches many of the best, like Barbara, Ian, Peri and Sarah Jane Smith (my personal vote as best companion, most credible, and also well played). What shows up her strength is not simply the individual things she does, but the *development* of her personality, as a result of her experiences. So we should acknowledge Billie Piper's success in projecting the rôle, which has strengthened the credibility of the character.

Also, it is not irrelevant that, at the climax of the first story, it is the Doctor who faces 'certain death' and the companion who saves him, not the reverse. No doubt this is another reason the story is called *Rose*.

So, to look at Rose (and Adam and Jack, not to mention earlier companions) is to see different ways of being a companion – or, to look at this from a different angle, different ways of being a 'disciple'. We shall see how Adam failed in Chapter 9: unlike Judas Iscariot, he did not betray *deliberately*, but the terrible consequences of his greed still showed a betrayal of his rôle. Symbolically, the companion often represents the viewer: What would it be like for *us* to enter the dangerous world of the Doctor? So this series enables us to ask ourselves: What sort of companions would we be? When, at the end of *The Time Meddler*, companion Stephen Taylor said he liked the idea of being a 'crew-member' aboard the TARDIS, Vicki quickly corrected him. Pointing to the Doctor, she said, 'He's the crew; we're just the passengers.' This was the original Doctor's view. But later Doctors involved their companions, better matching the parallel with Jesus, who said that his disciples were not to be servants, who don't understand their master's business. 'Instead I have called you friends, for everything that I learned from my Father I have made known to you' (John 15:15). If we are crew, what will we do?

Afterthought: What sort of a companion to the Doctor would you be?

3

The Evil of the Universe

Danger, Doctor, danger!

Doctor Who is an adventure series, and in most stories, the Doctor and his companions face dangers caused by evil. Occasionally there are other dangers, like the threat of being eaten by terrible 'animals' (Drashigs in *Carnival of Monsters*, a giant cat in *Planet of Giants*), or other natural or extra-ordinary hazards. One early example saw the TARDIS being sucked back in time towards the destructiveness of the beginning of time (*The Edge of Destruction*). But mostly, the dangers are caused by the TARDIS crew up against *evils* of one kind or another.

What is evil? What causes it? And how should we face up to it? The nature of the evil faced in *Doctor Who* varies enormously, and it is not always what it seems. In *The Daleks*, the crew sort out the easy question of who to trust: the menacing, machine-like 'Dalek people', or the almost Scandinavian-like peaceable, humanoid Thals. But on the doomed planet of *Galaxy 4*, the threat comes not from the hideous, reportedly violent, methane-breathing Rills, but from the glamorous female Drahvins. And in *The Mind Robber*, the character causing all their dangers (the Author) is discovered to be as much a victim of the ultimate problem as the Doctor and his companions are.

So there is a great richness about the variety of challenges the Doctor faces. Meanwhile, unlike James Bond (who simply unmasks and defeats villainy, often with weapons), the Doctor rarely uses weapons but tries to outwit his opponents and, more than that, to *think* his way through to solve his problems. He doesn't always succeed in his strategies, however. In *Rose* and most other stories of the new series, he needed Rose or others to save him.

But this is what makes *Doctor Who* so different from *Star Trek, Star Wars, Babylon 5, Farscape, Stargate SG-1, Blakes 7* and so many others. In these stories, the heroes are routinely armed, and as often as not military heroes (whether for or against the governing 'Federation' etc.). But the Doctor is generally unarmed and normally refuses to kill, even if that leaves him ridiculously vulnerable. The First Doctor made it clear early on that he would never kill, except where immediately necessary to save his own life. Perhaps the Doctor being an unarmed hero reflects a distinctively British attitude, which likes to think of its police as unarmed – and recoils at 'shoot to kill' orders.

So the Doctor tackles the evils of the universe, not with violence (though he may often 'reverse the polarities' and enable the villains' own violence to be redirected back at themselves), but with thoughtfulness and compassion, outwitting the complexities and deceits of the forces of evil, and saving those endangered by them. This requires a different strategy and course every time.

What this means is that most stories will reveal some evil to be faced, and always a dangerous challenge. Each story of the new series exposes these challenges, and reveals some facet of the nature of evil, and the appropriate response to it. So in this book, we will find ourselves looking at the nature of the evil, time and again, and discover not only the different forms it takes, but also the varied problems it raises, and explore the appropriate responses we could make to it.

The first story of the new series introduced us to an old foe: the Autons.

Who are the Autons?

The villains of the first story are the Autons (though they are not named as such). For a fan of the classic series of *Doctor Who*, the episode *Rose* is uncannily like a much faster-paced version of the first story of the Third Doctor, *Spearhead From Space* (1970), even to the point of an implied regeneration, with the Doctor adjusting to his new appearance (here abbreviated to two seconds as he looks in a mirror and comments on his ears). The similarity with the earlier story is so close it must be deliberate. Mannequins smashing shop-windows as the Autons attempt to take over the planet – an iconic sequence from the classic series – is repeated here. And the story is very fast-paced, with the original 85-minute story squeezed into 40 minutes. A choice has been made to ensure pace and action. What is arguably lost is some of the sense of suspense which a slower build-up enabled. But maybe as the series gets established, writers will feel able to take the time to build a strong sense of menace and suspense.

The Autons have featured before in the world of *Doctor Who*. Most notably, a year after their introduction they were the key menace in the story that introduced the Doctor's nemesis, the Master (*Terror of the Autons*). Also, in the long gap between the last TV episode, *Survival*, in 1989, and *Rose*, there were many spin-off video stories produced, of which the best were probably the *Auton* trilogy (*Auton*, 1998; *Auton: Sentinel*, 1999; and *Auton: Awakening*, 2000) – a trilogy with very much an *X-Files* feel to it.

What is the Nestene threat?

1. Behind everything else is the 'Nestene Consciousness' – a living plastic entity. In *Spearhead from Space*, this is a form of collective consciousness. The Nestenes also engage in thought-control over the director of Auto Plastics. In *Rose*, the Consciousness controls plastic, not by radio waves, but by thought waves.

2. The automated, armed mannequins (Autons) – the main army of the Nestene Consciousness. In *Spearhead from Space*, they are named as Autons, products of Auto Plastics, which persuaded shops to switch to plastic mannequins – and *Madame Tussaud's* to accept plastic replicas. The armed mannequins in *Rose* imply a similar strategy.

3. The Nestenes can manipulate plastic, and animate it generally. In *Terror of the Autons*, children's plastic trolls, and even telephone cable and plastic sofas present lethal threats. In *Rose*, a wheelie bin can move and capture Rose's boyfriend, Mickey.

4. The Nestenes have the ability to manipulate plastic to achieve a more-or-less exact replica of a human being, as with Mickey. In *Spearhead from Space*, a facsimile human, Channing, takes over Auto Plastics. Over time, the Nestenes successfully replicate the entire government and army higher command.

The Autons, therefore, are the army of the Nestene Consciousness, which in each story is pictured as simply an invasion force, intending to eradicate humanity, the sentient species of Earth, and only real obstacle to invasion (apart from the Doctor!). In *Spearhead from Space*, this genocide would precede repopulating the planet with a new organic form suitable for living all over the planet, and inhabited by the Consciousness. In so doing, they are following a long pattern of colonising planets. In *Rose*, the Nestenes now need a new planet urgently because of a cosmic war which is referred to throughout this first new season.

Responding to the Auton threat

So the Auton threat is the basic one: a hostile alien species intent on wiping out the human race. But there is an unexpected twist in the response of the Doctor.

To the traditional *Doctor Who* fan, familiar with this history, the most surprising turn in *Rose* is where the Doctor enters the base of the Nestene Consciousness and attempts a diplomatic alternative to simple confrontation. This is a surprise in terms of previous responses to the Auton threat, but not in terms of the Doctor's way of handling the dangers of global invasion.

'I seek audience with the Nestene Consciousness under peaceful contract, according to convention 15 of the Shadow Proclamation.'

The Ninth Doctor, in *Rose*

The Third Doctor, in particular, often found himself trying to prevent war between civilisations by seeking a diplomatic compromise instead. In this he often failed, but many times succeeded. In *The Silurians* (1970), he tried to resolve a conflict between humans and a revived, long-dormant Earth-based reptilian species. While he won over some on both sides, hotheads (both human and Silurian) prevailed, and near fatal conflict broke out, the human race saved only by the Doctor's advanced path lab skills.

On other occasions, he succeeded. For example, he eventually outwitted his nemesis, the Master, by persuading humans and Draconians to resume peaceful relations in *The Frontier in Space* (1973). Also, he twice brought peace to medieval Peladon by encouraging forces of moderation and progress against those of reactionary prejudice and exploitation (*The Curse of Peladon*, 1972; *The Monster of Peladon*, 1974).

'Blessed are the peacemakers' (Matthew 5:9) is one of Jesus' controversial beatitudes. But it is closer to conventional wisdom now. *Securing* peace and reconciliation instead of vendetta and conquest is not so easy. Ensuring that bitter enemies learn to forgive and live together is vital, but very difficult to achieve. Yet Archbishop Tutu's Truth and Reconciliation Committee showed it can be done, and such peacemaking can play a major rôle in enabling a society to move on from vendetta and war to peace and reconciliation. The challenges during the Balkan wars of the 1990s, and the gradual improvement there since the Dayton Accord, show both how difficult and yet how important such diplomacy and peace-making is.

It is a measure of the subtlety of *Doctor Who* that this track in the struggle with evil is part of the score. Furthermore, scriptwriters have often avoided the cheap manoeuvre of simply having the Doctor attempt diplomacy, just to see him fail every time, to prove the intractable evil of his foes. Instead, he succeeds almost as often as he fails.

All this reminds us that evil may take over individuals and societies, but we should not demonise either. 'Our struggle is not against flesh and blood', Paul warned in Ephesians 6, 'but against the rulers, against the authorities, against the powers of this dark world and against the spiritual forces of evil in the heavenly realms.' In other words, we struggle *against* evil ideas, but *for* people; *against* the spiritual forces that inspire evil, but *for* the people, even if they become its agents – so we struggle for people even when they become our enemies. Our struggle is for them to be liberated from evil, as Jesus remarked in his utterly controversial challenge: 'Love your enemies' (Matthew 5:44).

The Doctor would prefer to persuade the Nestene Consciousness to abandon an invasion of Earth, and perhaps seek an alternative planet without sentient life instead. But he does not get very far with his diplomatic approach. The Nestene Consciousness is too distrustful of his superior TARDIS technology, and of his plastic-destroying 'insurance policy'. It advances its plan to wipe out the human race. In the chaos

that follows, through Rose's courage and skill, the Nestenes
are thwarted, and the Doctor, Rose, Mickey and Rose's mother
are all saved – though not before some carnage achieved by
Auton violence.

The Doctor killed the Nestene invaders to save the human
race. It was not his preferred solution – but his 'insurance
policy' of a lethal weapon showed he was not confident he
could persuade the Nestenes to abandon their invasion. And
he very nearly failed. His approach raises the recurring issue
in *Doctor Who* of whether it can be right to kill in order, for
example, to save life. This first appeared in the first story, *The
Tribe of Gum*, and has been a frequent challenge. And it is a
central issue in the second episode, *The End of the World*; so
we return to this recurring dilemma in Chapter 10. But the
next question, also raised in *The End of the World*, is the complex character – or characters! – of the Doctor.

Afterthought: How hard is it to aim at a diplomatic solution
when confronted by evil? How hard is it to forgive and seek
reconciliation? And is it a waste of time?

Studies of models of society show that those that allow for
forgiveness survive, unlike others.

4

Who Is the Doctor?

The edge of destruction

The week after *Rose* was transmitted was of course the time when Christopher Eccleston revealed he was going to be the shortest-lived TV Doctor in *Doctor Who*. So by the end of the second episode (*The End of the World*), I, and I expect many fans had even more reason to feel downbeat about the series. For by then we had the end of the Ninth Doctor, the end of the Earth, the end of the human race, and the end of the Time Lords, and therefore the end of a whole range of possibilities, as Russell T. Davies began to flesh out a new mythology for the back-story to *Doctor Who*.

Question: In *Doctor Who*, who killed the last human being?

As we have seen, the Doctor routinely does not carry a gun. If (as in *The Seeds of Doom*) he does, commentators rightly suggest that (for all the strengths of the story) the scriptwriter has confused *Doctor Who* with *The Avengers* or some other show. The new series has taken this dimension on board. One major reason for introducing the character of Captain Jack Harkness is to have a character other than the Doctor who can carry a weapon – and even that is a change from the original series, where, with the obvious exception of 'savage' Leela, the companion does not routinely wield weapons either. Even highlander Jamie McCrimmon does not generally solve his problems by sword or gun after he joins the Doctor.

So the surprising thing is (to answer the chapter's opening question) that it is the Doctor himself who (apparently) causes the death of 'the last human being' (the duplicitous villain, Lady Cassandra O'Brien dot Delta Seventeen) in *The End of the World*.[1] And it is the Doctor who threatens to blast the defence-less mutating 'last Dalek'. That raises an issue of when it might or might not be right to kill (an issue we return to in Chapter 10). It also raises the question of the personality of the Doctor. For those familiar with earlier Doctors, it makes this Ninth Doctor seem perhaps more similar to the Sixth Doctor than any other previous one. But we are getting ahead of ourselves.

Doctor Who?

Russell T. Davies initially chose to avoid the overplayed joke here, in which a companion asks 'Yes, but Doctor *Who?*' – and had Rose ask him 'Doctor What?' instead. But who is the Doctor? *The End of the World* raised that question in a new way.

In the mythology of *Doctor Who*, the Doctor is a uniquely

---

[1] I say 'apparently', as death is not always so final in science fiction as in real life! Cassandra is due to return in Season 2 of the new series, though whether this is after her (apparent) death, or whether time-travelling enables the Doctor and Rose to meet her earlier in her life, I don't know at the time of writing. See *Doctor Who Magazine #361* (October 2005), pp. 4f.

radical member of a race dubbed Time Lords, from the planet Gallifrey in the 'constellation' Kasterborous. Time Lords may look human, but they are quite distinct anatomically, having two hearts and a different pulse, a different breathing system, enabling them to survive gas attacks fatal to humans, but a blood system for which aspirin would be fatal. They have an ability to switch off their bodies so they can appear dead for hours, and, most famously of all, a capacity to regenerate. This is a trigger in the Time Lords' DNA (or equivalent) which ensures that after a conventional death, an extraordinary biological process is activated, an internal mechanism which engenders not only a new body but also to some considerable extent a new mind and personality.

The new Time Lord retains all his (or her) memories, and there remains a considerable degree of continuity of overall personality, so the Doctor is consistently a hero throughout his regenerations, and the Master was a suave, sophisticated villain through *his* many regenerations. But there are substantial differences, which we will outline.

In *The Three Doctors* (1973), the First Doctor (as played by Hartnell) made a final appearance, and described the Third and Second Doctors respectively: 'Hmm? Oh, so you're my replacements, eh? A dandy and a clown!' The ten Doctors have varied not only in appearance, but also in temperament, personality, and even to some extent in morality.

The ten doctors

No, not a story you haven't seen (or not yet!). A quick checklist on each Doctor, actor, personality, and quirks.

1. An elderly Edwardian gent, played by William Hartnell (1963–66), he was pompous, stubborn, deeply private, and an anti-establishment scientific explorer and adventurer: 'a citizen of the Universe and a gentleman to boot!' (*The Daleks' Master Plan*).

2. An altogether more approachable and homely 'cosmic hobo', played by Patrick Troughton (1966–69). He was more consistently moral, and frequently he chaotically improvised his way out of crises, as when declaring 'I'm a genius!' to persuade an Ice Warrior not to kill him, but to use his skills. So he was also anti-establishment – but as a successful underdog.

3. More upright, both literally and metaphorically, played by Jon Pertwee (1970–74). Was he anti-establishment? Yes – in loathing bureaucracy, and in his charged sparring with the military mindset of Brigadier Lethbridge-Stewart and his UNIT[2] team. But he was rather more establishment than others, because of his UNIT alliance, and his teacher-like eagerness to correct the faults of all, displaying a hint of the First Doctor's arrogance, though differently. His was also the most James Bond-like Doctor, with gadgets, machines, races and soldiers aplenty.

4. Played by Tom Baker (1974–81), he was an eccentric, like the Second Doctor, though with something of the aloofness and arrogance of the First, but with a reckless sense of humour – poking fun at evil. Of the Daleks: 'If you're

[2] UNIT stands for United Nations Intelligence Taskforce – a small group of soldiers and scientists set up to tackle any possible alien or paranormal activity.

supposed to be "The Superior Race of the Universe", why don't you try climbing after me? Bye bye!' Of the Cybermen: 'You're just a pathetic bunch of tin soldiers skulking around the Galaxy in an ancient spaceship!'

5. The most straightforwardly upright Doctor, played by Peter Davison (1982–84) – a return to the style of the Third Doctor, but more uncomplicatedly compassionate – though with something of the humour of the Fourth Doctor, expressed differently, and a passion for cricket.

6. Like the Fourth Doctor, a complex Doctor, played by Colin Baker (1984–86). And despite the mistakenly brash costume,[3] he was darker, more arrogant even than the First Doctor, more pragmatic,[4] and more supercilious in his alien, supra-human perspectives.

7. Played by Sylvester McCoy (1987–96), he was both a charming clown, like the Second Doctor, and a schemer, like the First Doctor, only darker. This scheming was increasingly undertaken in an ambiguous way (this was pressed much harder in the *New Adventures of Doctor Who* novels in the 1990s). Incidentally Sylvester, with his soft Scottish accent, was the first to play the Doctor with an accent from 'North Britain'.

---

[3] Colin Baker himself (unsurprisingly) did not like this strange outfit. Actually he wanted something like Christopher Eccleston's! '. . . when John Nathan-Turner . . . asked me what I would like for a costume I asked for something unobtrusive and in all black. And what did I get? You don't know how lucky you were, Mr. E.' – *Dreamwatch #133* (October 2005), p. 85.

[4] 'Pragmatic' was the word the Sixth Doctor chose to differentiate himself from the Fifth and Seventh Doctors in the *Doctor Who Big Finish* audio story *The Sirens of Time*.

8. A much more straightforward Doctor, played by Paul McGann (in the film of 1996 and in audio stories since), presenting a return to something comparable to the Third Doctor, in an elegant and upright style, and with motor-cycle chases reminiscent of that era.

9. And so we come to the Ninth Doctor. Though he only saw one season (2005), the shape of his personality became pretty clear. Something of the almost shocking pragmatism of the Sixth Doctor returned, but without the assertive brashness (or costume); instead, there was more of the First Doctor's aloofness, which may have had more to do with his sense of survivor's guilt at uniquely surviving the end of his planet and race. This possibly also explains his sympathy for endangered races like the Gelth and even the Nestenes, as well as his consuming hatred of the 'last' Dalek. As for his anti-establishment credentials, he is not only 'from the north' but implicitly conveys a unique, working-class feel to the character. Previous Doctors were élite rebels; this rather different rebel was far more urban.

10. The Tenth Doctor, played by David Tennant (2005–?), is yet to come to screen at the time of writing. As the actor of Dr Briscoe in the new version of *The Quatermass Experiment*, before becoming the Doctor, Tennant continues the connection between that ground-breaking 1950s series and *Doctor Who* (visible especially in the heavy debt *The Daemons* owed to the third series, *Quatermass and the Pit*).

Regeneration, resurrection, incarnation

All forms of belief in life after death raise the question of the continuity of the personality. To what extent, if I experience life after death, will the 'I' who experiences the afterlife be the same person as the one who died? The Doctor's regenerations, his lives after deaths, raise this familiar religious question in a colourful way.

Now the way this is presented in *Doctor Who* reflects to some extent a Western version of **reincarnation** – after the end of life, starting a new life as someone else, but with (obscured) memories of a previous life. I say 'Western', because the Eastern belief, in religions like Buddhism and Hinduism, sees reincarnation more as a curse than a blessing. In Hinduism, samsara, the cycle of return, is the idea that we are condemned to keep returning to this life in ever new lives until we finally escape (by religious virtue) and achieve union with Brahman ('Universal Spirit'). Buddhism's vision of this has the goal as nirvana (usually translated as 'extinguishedness'). But Westerners (many New Agers and others), in a very supermarket-like attitude to religion, have added a very Western individualistic gloss, turning reincarnation from curse to hope. This pious wish would picture us living one life up to death, then starting another one afterwards, like Christopher Eccleston, after the difficulty of death, re-emerging as David Tennant. Perhaps a very desirable prospect! That wish is seductive, as it spares the individual from either the disturbing Christian challenge that life after death depends on our relationship with God, or the downbeat atheistic belief that we should abandon any hope of life after death.

Now the idea of reincarnation is very vulnerable to the problem of *continuity* of personality. What's more, it actually overlooks the way personality is developed; for a baby has a genetic legacy, and his or her personality is then shaped by experiences. The character of a newborn child is not random or disconnected from this legacy.

Of course, writers on *Doctor Who* often talk of a regeneration as for example the 'Tenth Incarnation' of the Doctor. What does it mean to talk not of a reincarnation, but an **incarnation**? Again, the atmosphere is more akin to a Western take on an Eastern idea – incarnation as an avatar. This makes the Doctor (if we pressed that in a religious way) more like a god-like epiphany! Should we think of the Doctor as a godlike immortal materialising into our world, before returning to the spiritual realm? The episode *Rose* has conspiracy theorist Clive suggesting this as a possible explanation of the way the Doctor seems to crop up in history. 'I think he's immortal.' (He then adds: 'I think he's an alien from another world.')

On the whole, *Doctor Who* resists going down this line – as far as the Doctor and his race are concerned. But it does not avoid the suggestion that we would meet godlike beings if we travelled with the Doctor – such entities as the 'Celestial Toymaker', the 'White Guardian', the 'Eternals' and the like. These are presented in various stories in the old series as immortals, godlike, but also moral, evil or amoral. These 'gods', super-human but flawed, are reminiscent of the gods of ancient Greece and Rome. If we could join the Doctor and cross the boundaries of time and space, would we be interrupted by such godlike entities?

It might be tempting to dismiss this idea in *Doctor Who* as primitive superstition repackaged as entertainment. But let us reflect on why people believed, or now believe, in such entities. This belief is rooted in human experience of powerful, often hostile forces at work in the world, forces like war, love, ageing, music, communication, death, and so on. And gods like Mars (war), Venus (love), Mercury (communication) and the rest reflected those fears in concrete form.

Yet for centuries we have rightly rejected that perspective. The world is not dominated by incarnations of godlike entities threatening our peace, or even saving us from disasters, but by cosmic forces at work in a universe that can be rationally understood. The origin of this belief in a rationally intelligible world, open to scientific enquiry, is found in the Bible – the world is not made up of star-gods, a Sun-god, a Moon-god and the rest. Genesis 1:16 declares that the sun, moon and stars are simply created things, made by God; they are not gods. The universe is created and ordered. So even if we could build a TARDIS and move through time and space we would still not encounter godlike beings, such as the Black Guardian. And neither should the Doctor himself be seen as an incarnation of a godlike entity.

Of course, the word 'incarnation' has an alternative, very Christian usage: the central Christian belief that Jesus is the incarnation of God. Does our previous questioning throw that into doubt? These superhuman gods are different. We will not encounter gods, independent of God. But Christians are confident that we can encounter God himself, and God makes himself known in a whole variety of ways – through prayer, in and through the words of the Bible, in unexpected thoughts, in and through the wonder of the universe, through other people, and above all in the person of Jesus himself, who we are convinced is the embodiment – or incarnation – of everything that God is.

We return to the question of life after death, and the idea of the Doctor regenerating as a picture of this. What if, instead of reincarnation, we see how the Doctor's regenerations might illustrate the Hebrew and Christian belief in personal **resurrection**? This is the idea that a person lives one life during which he or she develops a relationship with God – through Jesus Christ, as far as Christians are concerned. After death, the body dies, but at the end of time, God raises the believer to share with him and other believers in eternal life. This, too, raises the question of the continuity of personality, but in a different form. For Christians believe we shall not die, nor enter eternal life simply as a spirit being absorbed into some greater whole. Instead, the belief in resurrection implies a personal life with a bodily dimension, which, though different in key ways to life here and now, is also in continuity with it, both bodily and spiritually.

The differences are that life now is a life with degeneration towards death, whereas eternal life isn't. Life as we know it can't avoid death; but resurrected life will not be mortal. Life now includes the need for procreation, but eternal life won't; instead, as Jesus said, we shall 'be like the angels' (Matthew 22:30). Life now includes the fact that we continue to do unkind, sinful or even evil deeds. But this will not happen in the resurrected life. And to that extent, therefore, our personalities will be different, purified of all sin.

Obviously when the Doctor regenerates, for example from Sylvester McCoy (Seventh Doctor) to Paul McGann (Eighth

Doctor) – in the film of 1996 – he does not change in these ways. The Eighth Doctor is not immortal, can't avoid ageing, or sin. But as a metaphor for life after death as resurrection, is it helpful?

The biblical Christian understanding of life after death, as we have seen, clearly includes elements of continuity and discontinuity between life as we know it now and life after death. But how does this work out in practice?

In reality, there are many unanswered questions bound up with this. For example, will we remember all that happened in our human life, including all our sins, or will the perfection of heaven mean we forget them? I can remember the shock when I heard my (unconventional) Christian youth leader suggesting the latter, and that we would also forget anyone who was not going to be in heaven, otherwise heaven would be marred by longings of missing them. I am reminded of a scene in *The Five Doctors*, when the Doctor's earlier 'incarnations' are being attacked and captured from different time streams. As each one is kidnapped, the Fifth Doctor feels the loss as if he has suddenly lost all the memories of his time as that Doctor: 'A man is the sum of his memories, you know – a Time Lord even more so.'

Would the perfection of heaven mean a similar loss of memories? And if I had lost all those memories, would I still be the same person? In practice, we can make some headway with this question by looking at a comparable situation in *this* life – when people carry terrible memories, what can they do to try to get to a place of healing? Most commonly, people try either to gain revenge, or else to forget. Revenge may be the aim, but no amount of revenge ever satisfies, because it doesn't take the pain away and doesn't heal. So the other common approach is trying to forget, and simply move on. Sometimes this succeeds. Often the success is at best partial and impermanent.

But there is a better way. In the last chapter, we reminded ourselves of the South African model of facing these painful memories positively, rather than forgetting – by a process of forgiveness. And that collective experiment can be attempted for the individual. People with experience of counselling, prayer ministry, and other therapeutic approaches find that sometimes a person can be helped genuinely and truly to move on. They don't usually completely forget their painful experiences, but they do find that these no longer hold their destructive power. Instead, they come to a place of genuine healing and personal recovery. My suspicion is that our experience in heaven will be something a bit more like that. We will not be stripped of our memories. But because of the healing power of eternal life, memories will no longer have the destructive power they once did. So there will be continuity of personality, but discontinuity in the destructive dimensions of our experience.

5

The Occult Universe of Doctor Who

A ghost story, not with Ebenezer Scrooge, or the ghost of Christmas yet to come, but with Charles Dickens himself? That is what the episode *The Unquiet Dead* provides us with. But things have a habit of not being quite what they seem in *Doctor Who*, and this is certainly true with ghosts and other occult and paranormal phenomena. In *The Smugglers*, the Doctor is even prepared to make a Tarot reading from playing cards; whether this is simply a ruse to distract his guard and so escape, or whether he actually believes his reading he leaves unanswered, but with enough ambiguity to suggest both. So prepare to enter the strange, occult universe of the Doctor, with ghosts, séances, Ouija, the devil himself, all real – and yet not paranormal at all, but extraterrestrial.

Visiting your historical heroes

Doctor Who frequently escorts us into history, and the Doctor often tells us he has met famous characters from the past. In *The Unquiet Dead*, we get to see one of those encounters.

What would it be like to meet Charles Dickens? The Ninth Doctor is chuffed, and reacts almost like a schoolboy meeting his hero. Perhaps if the Fifth Doctor could have met cricketing legend W.G. Grace we would have had a similar reaction. Later, however, the Doctor is not beyond belittling Dickens, and reminds us more of the First Doctor, who treated himself as equal if not superior to every legend, frequently coming off badly as a result! He gambled with Emperor Kublai Khan (in *Marco Polo* – and lost the TARDIS!), and posed as the god Zeus to Agamemnon and Achilles – and when this impersonation failed, dreamed up the Trojan Horse idea to keep his Greek captors impressed (*The Myth Makers*).

I thought the historical touches in *The Unquiet Dead* were well done, and gave the audience something of the feel of what it would be like to enter Victorian Wales, noting for example that Gwyneth when discussing school has a different understanding to Rose of what it is. For she would have been educated (before universal schooling) in a Sunday school, no doubt provided by one of the chapels, through which children were taught reading, writing and sums, as well as religious lessons.

The earliest *Doctor Who* stories alternated science fiction stories with purely historical ones, in which the Doctor and companions would encounter Napoleon, Nero, Richard the Lionheart and others. However, since the First Doctor there have been only two purely historical stories (*The Highlanders* in 1966–67 and *Black Orchid* in 1982). Instead, most *Doctor Who* stories set in the past have included a science fiction element – for example, the Daleks entering Victorian Britain through static-electricity experiments gone wrong (*The Evil of* the Daleks). One of the best of those was *The Time Warrior*, which saw a Sontaran stranded in medieval England and meddling brilliantly in local feuding (1973–74). Some stories, from as early as *The Aztecs* (1964) onwards, raised the potential of the abuse of the power in time travelling, expanded since *The Time Monster* (1973) with the problems of dangerous creatures of the time vortex. These issues are centre stage in *Father's Day* and *The Long Game* – which we will explore in Chapter 9.

Meanwhile, those who liked *The Unquiet Dead*, with its pseudo-séance, would probably also like *The Daemons* (1972) and *Image of the Fendahl* (1977). For *The Unquiet Dead* follows a long tradition in *Doctor Who* of taking the paranormal as real, but alien-induced phenomena. This raises the biggest question in this episode for those reflecting on the social, ethical and religious issues in *Doctor Who*: What should we make of ghosts and the like?

Ghost light?

How should we think about paranormal phenomena? As far as science fiction and fantasy TV is concerned, the extraordinary series *The X-Files* changed the way some happenings are understood, certainly the way they are imagined in science fiction. But first we need to see where the ghost story came from.

Actually, setting the story *The Unquiet Dead* in 1869 is very astute, for the ghost story is a very nineteenth-century phenomenon, and many of the enduring images we have of it, and of the related horror story genre, stem from that time – such as

Mary Shelley's *Frankenstein* (1818) and Bram Stoker's *Dracula* (1897), not to mention early nineteenth-century writer Edgar Allen Poe's many stories. And we should of course not forget Charles Dickens himself, whose *Christmas Carol* (1843) is, if anything, an even more celebrated ghost story, and was indeed the story 'Dickens' was retelling when interrupted by the ghostly Mrs Redpath.

What happened in the nineteenth and twentieth centuries is a new take on an old set of issues: what to make of the spiritually 'weird'.

By the weird, I mean the whole range of occult, paranormal, parapsychological experiences, and so on, such as claims to communicate with spirits of the dead, and with other spirits, claims to have seen such 'ghosts' or spirits, claims to be able to read minds, tell the future, claims to be able to fly on broomsticks or on animals, claims to be able to control minds and claims to strange celestial secrets, or other secret powers, powers to curse or to release from curse, and so on.

Very broadly, attitudes to these phenomena have gone through several phases over the past 15 centuries. In what we misleadingly call the Dark Ages, or perhaps better the Early Middle Ages (say, AD 500–1300), a healthy scepticism was the norm. There are people who make such claims; however, we should not take them at face value but as spiritually induced illusions. The Christian writers said we should beware such pagan spirituality.

We see several changes late in the Middle Ages, during the Renaissance era. One development was the renaissance of classical (i.e. pagan) antiquity, which included growth of interest in 'secret wisdom' in gnosticism, cabbalism, astrology, alchemy and the like among many intellectuals – the occult sciences. (*Doctor Who's* take on this is seen best in *The Masque of Mandragora*.) Alongside this, deviant ideas, groups and practices began to flourish. But many were seen as a threat to powerful interests in church and state, and were suppressed with increasing ruthlessness. These included alleged heretics, Jews and 'witches', persecution of all of whom grew apace from the fourteenth century onwards. And third, from the 1480s onwards, we see a more rationalist mind-set developing, which takes completely literally the claims of witches (pagan spiritists, herbal abortionists, etc.) to be able to fly on broomsticks. As a result, they are perceived as satanic witches in pursuit of a witches' Sabbath, which grandiose conspiracy theory sparks the mania for burning people for witchcraft. Actually, this craze developed strongest everywhere where education advanced, and was pursued most fiercely by the most educated, secular authorities.[1]

Gradually, first with a few sane voices – even at the height of the craze – and later by everyone, the murderous folly of all this was recognised, and reformers first called for a return to the sober scepticism of the so-called Dark Ages. Later, as the secularising spirit of the Enlightenment took hold in the eighteenth century, a rejection of *all* religious intensity ('enthusiasm') became fashionable among the cultured classes, and

---

[1] Those keen to see the evidence for this analysis should read *Early Modern European Witchcraft. Centres and Peripheries* ed. by Gustav Henningsen and Bengt Ankarloo (1987) translated from Swedish, Estonian, Danish, and other languages (Clarendon Press, 1990).

the whole episode was treated as a wave of primitive superstition.

So by the start of the nineteenth century, a new attitude held sway: occult phenomena and in particular those associated with 'witchcraft' were seen to be a load of impossible nonsense. Judges, witnesses and mobs, who believed in them and sent alleged witches to their deaths, were treated as victims of the basest superstition. A new myth of the rise of modern science reigned supreme – and deviations from this were suppressed. One example is Isaac Newton's profound commitment to alchemy; alchemy formed 10 per cent of his library and was the subject of many of his writings and experiments, but these were all censored from his mid-nineteenth-century *Complete Works*, being published only in the last 40 years or so.

Therefore for the nineteenth century, all talk of witches, spirits, broomsticks and so on was pure mumbo-jumbo. And so now, safely treated as imaginary, it was in a position to be reinvented as a work of a novelist's imagination, as fiction, as make-believe. This could be in children's fairy tales, where witches were now complete fantasy figures who flew on broomsticks, talked with animals, etc. It was now taken as pure make-believe, not satanic conspiracy. Or, as we have seen, it could be reinvented in the darker genres of ghost stories and horror.

In addition, a quite different nineteenth-century development saw the rise of new spiritual movements like spiritualism, Mary Baker Eddy's Christian Science and the Theosophy of Hélèna Blavastky and Annie Besant, which first talked of a 'New Age of Aquarius' in the nineteenth century.

However, in the last 40 years, a new, more postmodern scepticism has grown, which takes apart this comfortable science-based grand story and questions the certainties of nineteenth-century science and history. Historians of the witch-burning craze now suggest that what may have been happening was not the complete nonsense assumed 100 years ago, nor the diabolical conspiracy assumed at the time, but that witches reporting experiences of flying and the rest of it were recounting the results of trance-state experiences, which seemed true and real to them.

Now as we have said, the *X-Files* took up this new mood strongly, pressing the suggestion as far as it could that maybe there was something genuinely going on in paranormal experience, something truly supernatural. However, *Doctor Who* is rooted in an earlier era, where the assumption was that there would be a rational explanation for all occult phenomena. What *Doctor Who* does (like *Star Trek*, and *Star Trek: The Next Generation*, though not later *Star Trek* series) is to assume a science fiction variation: the occult phenomena, whether ghosts (*Image of the Fendahl*) Ouija (*Timelash*), tarot readings (*The Smugglers*), the Devil (*The Daemons*), Satan – alias Sutekh (*Pyramids of Mars*), or now, effective séances (*The Unquiet Dead*), are only 'otherworldly' by being caused by aliens.

This still places *Doctor Who* with earlier SF, which simply saw occult phenomena as utter fantasy, and completely incredible, and not, for example, with the *X-Files*, which pursues the 'what if?' factor: what if the paranormal, the spiritually dark presented *real* dangers? The only faint hint of this more deliberately ambiguous approach in *The Unquiet Dead* comes in a piece of dialogue towards the end, where the Doctor tries to explain why Gwyneth was beyond saving. But how could she be as already dead as the Doctor claims, if she somehow still had the will to cause her body (if we may speak that way) to light the match which 'saved the world'?

> 'There are more things in heaven and earth than are dreamt of in your philosophy – *even for you, Doctor!'*
>
> 'Charles Dickens' reapplying Shakespeare in
> *The Unquiet Dead*

'Dickens' might seem to be implying that since the facts did not add up, there was a genuine supernatural mystery, perhaps that an already dead Gwyneth somehow *did* act. . .

So are ghosts just mumbo-jumbo?

So if we are in a time when we can start asking again if there really is anything in this whole world of ghosts, spirits and devils, how can we make sensible progress without repeating mistakes of the past?

Surprisingly, Christians in the West are probably just as likely to disbelieve in the reality of ghosts and the rest as nonreligious people, despite the fact that there is more than a hint of their reality in the Bible.

The basic approach in the Bible – consistently in Old and New Testaments – is that the attempt to communicate with the dead is not so much mumbo-jumbo as a forbidden area. And the reason it is forbidden is that people who disobey seem to get tangled up with dark spiritual forces that are real, and are opposed by – and indeed opposed to – God. The clearest example of this is the sorry tale of Saul, Israel's first king, a man of great spiritual sensitivity, but not equal wisdom. He had originally banned mediums and spiritists from the land. But now, desperate for a message of hope, he turns to a witch at Endor, and asks her to act as a medium to bring up the deceased prophet Samuel. The text of the Bible in 1 Samuel 28 tells of a surprising development: she succeeds in a way. However, there is a strong hint that she is genuinely shocked by the way things transpire, as if what actually happens is quite different to what she had expected. In other words, it is as if God has somehow allowed this banned experiment of spiritualism to succeed, so that Samuel may indeed be allowed to speak one more time: to declare God's judgement against Saul.

In some ways, this passage is the most exceptional in the whole of the Bible on the subject of communicating with the dead. Much of the Old Testament expresses a cautious un-certainty about life after death, as revelation about it was yet to be given. So Ezekiel, questioned by God perhaps c.575 BC about whether a great army of skeletons can live again, replies simply, 'O Sovereign Lord, you alone know' (Ezekiel 37:3). Meanwhile, the latest parts of the Old Testament, and the New Testament generally, tell of life after death not as anything to do with ghosts, but as an act of God in raising the dead to a new, immortal, non-corruptible resurrection body (e.g. 1 Corinthians 15:25–54).

But the Bible is far from denying the reality of a spiritual realm, or from asserting that the only error of mediums and spiritists is treating fantasy as reality. The core belief of prophets and other believers in the Bible is that mediums and spiritists present a dangerous and misleading illusion, which is a no-go area for believers, because it represents the attempt to gain spiritual power or knowledge apart from God. For example, Isaiah comments: 'When men tell you to consult mediums and spiritists, who whisper and mutter, should not a people enquire of their God? Why consult the dead on behalf of the living?' (Isaiah 8:19).

Furthermore, the Bible is clear that there is a dark and dangerous side to spirits and spiritism. The Old Testament talks in terms of an injurious spirit, and the New in terms of an unclean spirit (often translated as evil spirit), and the implication is that those who seek contact with spirits which are independent of God are asking for trouble. Jesus himself engages in a ministry of healing which includes freeing people from these dark forces. While it is a mistake to assume that people generally are affected by such devious spirits (Jesus' healing involves freeing people from such evil only in a minority of cases), or that the New Testament presumes psychological conditions are generally caused by evil spirits, it does imply that spiritual problems are real and can have a deep and destructive effect on some individuals. And deliberate openness to spiritual powers other than God is the most obvious cause of such dangers.

Now if there were no spiritual power or effect in séances, Ouija and the rest, and they were pure fantasy, then of course there would be no problem in treating them as fantasy ideas. But if there *is* a reality to any of this, then it would be a dangerous mistake to treat the issue flippantly.

Having said that, today's teenagers – Christian or otherwise

– are pretty sophisticated, and it may be that a youth leader might feel there was some benefit in being controversial and raising the issue of spiritual powers and how to think about them from this starting-point. The scene in *The Unquiet Dead* where the Doctor calls the somewhat psychic and telepathic Gwyneth to act as a medium – not for the spirits of the departed (as in a conventional séance) but to call up these gaseous aliens – could be the basis for a discussion on the spiritual world.

Discussion: In a séance, do you think you are more likely to encounter gaseous aliens, spirits of dead people, evil spirits pretending to be the dead, or nothing real at all, just trickery or psychological self-deception?

Why does the Bible warn against such practices?

6

Doctor Who After 9/11

With three full episodes devoted to their felonious exploits in season one of the new series, the nefarious Slitheen present several new angles on the nature of evil, and we will explore two of them in this chapter, arising from their character and their threat.

Who are the Slitheen?

The Slitheen turn out not to be an alien species, but just a family from a species (which is a new species to *Doctor Who*). In *Aliens of London*, they assume the disguises of leading members of government, civil service, the army, and so on, consuming their victims in the process. They are led by the one disguised as Acting Prime Minister Joseph Green.

Their repeated flatulence (explained by the release of gases attendant on the awkwardness of compressing their bodies inside the human form), not to mention the burping of the Nestene-activated dustbin in *Rose*, is perhaps the most obvious outward indication of the way in which new *Doctor Who* has something more of the feel of *Farscape* about it. And as we will see (in Chapter 13), the TARDIS also feels quite a bit nearer to 'Moya', the organic spaceship of *Farscape*, than *Doctor Who* of the 1960s. But a better lesson from *Farscape*, helping it to sustain longer storylines in an era where viewer loyalty is less secure, is their 'previously on *Farscape*' feature, which picks up key moments of whichever earlier episodes are relevant. *Aliens of London* did this by reminding us of Rose's family before she returned – a year late!

But the most interesting and unusual feature about the Slitheen is that they are *not* an alien species, but only a family from one. *Boom Town* takes their story further, and reveals they are wanted criminals on their home planet.

Up to now, most villains in *Doctor Who* have been either individuals, or whole species. So the idea of a family of villains is a new departure. Family is very much the secondary undercurrent of the two-parter, *Aliens of London* and *World War III*, as the story covers not only the Slitheen family but also Rose's. Rather like Tony Blair's advisor Alastair Campbell saying, 'We don't do "God",' the Doctor says, 'I don't do "domestic".' But he seems to find it harder to avoid than he would like.

What are we to make of the idea of a *family* of villains? Many people – whether Christian or not – tend to see the family as the best bulwark against moral and social decay.

Parenthood is a key part of this. For many people, when they first become parents, it brings a real spark of something new in their lives: for the first time, they move beyond living lives revolving largely around themselves and their selfish interests, to a new focus, the spark of compassion, a focus of genuinely caring for someone other than themselves. Of course, that's not true for all. Some passionately care for others whether they become parents or not; and some people, even when they become parents, do not essentially escape the self-centredness of their lives. Instead, they simply add children to their list of self-centred interests, or worse still, treat children as an imposition, resenting the new restrictions on an otherwise unrestrained self-centred lifestyle.

But despite such exceptions, it remains true that for many people, parenthood provides a spark to a new dimension of other-centredness. No doubt this is one important reason why we instinctively feel the family is a force for moral good in society. So, to those of us who think in such terms, the family Slitheen is a bit of a slap in the face.

How *can* the family go so wrong? A deeper and more careful enquiry into the human race reminds us of human families similarly engaged in evil. For the family Slitheen are a kind of Mafia, whose 'godfather' is Jocrassa Fel Fotch Passameer-Day Slitheen (disguised as Acting PM Green). They tell the Doctor, 'Slitheen is our surname.'

Now, the members of a family can root for each other in a compassionate way. However, in our broken, fallen world, this family dimension can also be corrupted: it can become a conspiracy, as family members root for each other *against* the rest of the world.

This problem should actually be no surprise for Christians who believe in the Fall – that the good world God made is fractured by sin and evil, that the world as we experience it is not one in perfect harmony, but every aspect of it is fallen, and vulnerable to corruption. So everything we do can have its good side, or can be used for evil instead. Family is therefore not *always* a force for good. It, too, can be corrupted.

Doctor Who usually paints evil in primary colours, vivid and clear. So the evil of the family Slitheen is on the grand scale – to destroy every living creature on planet Earth, just to make money during a recession. Closer to home, the Mafia has provided a human example of families conspiring together, with a readiness to murder for financial gain. But these extreme examples can act as a vivid reminder to us all that it's not family as such, but the way we 'do family' that provides a force for good – or evil. Where we root for family and therefore *against* society, in a small way, we are following the conspiratorial example of the Slitheen.

Discussion: Is Rose's mother, Jackie, treating 'family' in a selfish way, when she implores the Doctor to take no risks with Rose's life, when he needs to save the world? Or is her compassion for Rose the root of Rose's caring, helping her to be ready to risk her life to save others?

Doctor Who in the twenty-first century

The rather cheeky take on Tony Blair's Iraq policy – during the 2005 election campaign – with an 'Acting Prime Minister' bogusly declaring we must have UN authorisation for nuclear weapons because WMD may be used 'within 45 seconds' neatly opens up the issues of *Doctor Who* in the twenty-first century.

Doctor Who is an adventure in space and time, and to children during the space race in the 1960s, the dreams of science fiction were coming true. The twenty-first century seemed to promise a new world, and *Doctor Who* could transport us there.

The twenty-first century has now arrived, of course. What aspects did it get right and wrong? Not just the technical changes, but social change?

Doctor Who writers and fans are not the same as those of *Star Trek*, of course. 'Trekkers' are keen to point to the incidental scientific and technical prescience of the show, commenting on how the communicator has arrived as the mobile phone (though less keen to tell us when the transporters will be able to teleport human beings!). But 'Whovians' do not promise the discovery of taranium, fluid links or even time travel.

That said, there is nonetheless a great deal of picturing the near future in *Doctor Who*. It does it nicely in incidental ways – already in the first episode, *An Unearthly Child*, where Ian and Barbara struggle to make sense of Susan Foreman, who unbeknown to them is an extraterrestrial time traveller from another world and time, as she stumbles in answer to a simple question about British currency. Embarrassed, she lets slip, 'Yes of course, the decimal system hasn't started yet.' This was a prophetic tease in 1963 as Britain used pounds, shillings and pence. But decimalisation was to come in 1971. Susan was only eight years out (a small error in time travel!), and *Doctor Who* correctly predicted this change would occur soon. Other changes were less accurate. *Doctor Who* (and many people, generally) assumed that the space race would continue indefinitely with the same intensity – and spending – after the Moon landing. *The Ambassadors of Death* had manned (British!) probes to Mars in 1971 according to Jean-Marc Lofficier's *Terrestrial Index* (the nearest thing to an official *Doctor Who* time-line). This shows manned flight to Jupiter by 1977 (*The Android Invasion*), and even (with one way of counting the date anyway) colonising of the interstellar planet Vulcan by 2020 (*Power of the Daleks*).[1] But that didn't happen. From our current perspective, human travel to the stars, or even to the outer planets, looks far less likely to happen this century than was expected 40 years ago.

But what about deeper changes? *Doctor Who* is nothing if not an adventure series, which sees our hero (with companion/s to protect) facing a succession of dangers, disasters and evil perils. By the Sixth and Seventh Doctors, the Doctor can rattle off a series of alien dangers to disturb the complacency of bureaucrats (a typical *Doctor Who* target). The Sixth Doctor berates the Time Lords for being corrupted by evil instead of battling against 'power-mad conspirators'. And the Seventh Doctor has a similar uphill struggle – against the myopia of the military mind:

'Daleks, Sontarans, Cybermen! – they're still in the nursery compared to us!'

The Sixth Doctor, in *The Trial of a Time Lord*

'I just want to say three things. . . Yeti, Autons, Daleks! – Cybermen and Silurians!'

The Seventh Doctor, in *Battlefield*

---

[1] Jean-Marc Lofficier: *Doctor Who – The Terrestrial Index* (Virgin: Target, 1991), pp.47, 56.

The world of *Doctor Who* is one in constant danger of disaster from monsters, villains, and fools. But how realistic is it or was it to see danger in terms of such archetypally mindless villains? I'm reminded of the *Not Only . . . But Also* sketch of Peter Cook and Dudley Moore in their spoof of Gerry Anderson's puppet series, all rolled into one: 'SuperThunderStingCar is Go!' And especially their villain, merging MasterSpy and the Hood as 'MasterBrawn'. 'First you blow up Anne Hathaway's cottage, now the Houses of Parliament. What next?!' – followed by evil laughter. In the memorable phrase of Douglas Adams, these villains are people who want to destroy the world 'for no good reason'.

The mindless rogues in *Doctor Who* are up there, among the features dismissed as the more laughable elements of the old series, along with cheap special effects, wobbly sets, screaming girls and unconvincing monsters. But as the twenty-first century gets underway, has this central element of *Doctor Who's* picture of the future proved right after all?

Politically, the twenty-first century started on the 11th September 2001. It may seem hard to remember it, but at the beginning of his presidency, George Bush was not proclaiming the neo-con vision of heavy intervention in other countries like Afghanistan, Iraq and Israel/Palestine. In fact, he was far more keen on a different Republican response: a degree of isolationism. He was not going to repeat Bill Clinton's hands-on attempt to solve other nations' crises. Camp David had not worked, and his America would back off from nation-building. But 9/11 changed all that.

Osama bin Laden. Here was someone who wanted to destroy the world 'for no good reason'. No good reason at least as far as the West was concerned. And at one level, the twenty-first century started with the classic nightmare of *Doctor Who* a reality. Suddenly those features behind many a *Doctor Who* story of the villain devising destructive plots are now regular news. In 2004, the UK government faced criticism that its counter-terrorism measures tore up eight centuries of liberty from Magna Carta onwards. In 2005, after the London bombings, the criticisms became muted, and the counter-terrorism measures sharper, as we learned of people who want to destroy us 'for no good reason'.

This also lay behind the case our Prime Minister put for the war in Iraq. There was the implication that bin Laden was in league with Saddam, and that without war, British people would within 45 minutes come under attack from Weapons of Mass Destruction – shorthand for nuclear destruction, biological plagues or massive chemical attack. Readers will have mixed ideas about the politics of intervention in Iraq, especially as it has developed. But what is clear is the relevance, even newsworthiness of that old *Doctor Who* idea of an enemy out there which wants to destroy the existing world, not quite for no good reason but because they want to destroy the current world order and rebuild the world according to *their* dreams.

But that was always there in *Doctor Who*, too. Most obviously, Davros in *Genesis of the Daleks* wanted to change the future for his humanoid race, and recast his people by means of genetic engineering into the Dalek race. And it's also there in the implied back-story to the Cybermen, and half-implied in the origins of the Sontarans.

But *Doctor Who* missed a trick. Back in the twentieth

century, it missed a trick. Almost always, the villains are conceived as either mad scientists, megalomaniacs – or both. But when we look at Osama bin Laden and his cohorts, and his imitators in Iraq and elsewhere, we see not mad scientists, and not even – or not primarily – megalomaniacs. Their inspiration comes from a very specific *religious* vision. It may be one rejected by most people in the world, including most Muslims, but it is motivated by religion, not science.

Question: In which *Doctor Who* story (from the classic series) does the Doctor fail to save the Earth and the people on it?

In *Doctor Who*, the scientists are often blinded by the desire to see their dangerous ideas implemented – blinded by personal hubris. This is what happens in *Inferno*, where the Doctor fails to save the Earth. This is a 'parallel Universe' Earth, where scientist Stahlmann is determined to complete his drilling project against the warning of the Doctor, and does so. As we have seen, the Doctor also failed to stop Davros willingly sacrificing his own entire Kaled race, just to see his precious Daleks succeed. The implied origin of the Cybermen sees these post-human monsters having arisen because earlier scientists on Mondas pressed cyborg and cybernetic developments beyond the point of no return.

Meanwhile, in *The Silurians*, humanity is threatened by biological WMD on account of a new genocidal, power-hungry leader of the sentient reptilians, so we could continue this list for a long time!

But where religion appears in *Doctor Who*, it's mostly a

throw-back to primitivism – or set in a genuinely medieval or earlier society. For example, in *The Power of Kroll*, the primitive Swampies have regressed to worshipping the fearful monster. Typically, such worship is introduced as a plot device, so that the Doctor's companion can be sentenced to endure human sacrifice at the end of the episode.

But religion of a different kind lies behind both the genuine threats and the rumours of threats that are shaping our societies and lives in the early years of the real twenty-first century. So how, realistically, could a *Doctor Who* story introduce this element in a viable way? This issue is both politically and culturally so sensitive that it would be hard to imagine adult drama doing justice to it. How could *Doctor Who*, which traditionally aims at a whole family audience, succeed?

The great advantage of *Doctor Who* as an adventure series with science fiction, fantasy, historical fiction, crime drama and so many other possibilities within its highly flexible format, is that it doesn't need to be too literal with this. For example, a story could envisage a visionary seeking to impose a 'Brave New World' type of society. A dangerous cult leader within a religion of an advanced people would be another example. The advantage of such scenarios is that the credibility of the villains is enhanced. If the villains have the understandable means of influencing people then a credibility gap is bridged. Hitler, after all, may not have been a conventional religious figure, but he was something of an occultic, mesmerising type, who regularly persuaded otherwise defeatist generals to continue the doomed war effort by such force of personality. Advanced religious aliens? *Doctor Who* has in its own way now given us a hint of an answer: Daleks chanting, 'Do not blaspheme!'

Doctor Who has in my opinion always been far stronger when its villains are believable, and that includes in their motives. Not for nothing is *Genesis of the Daleks* the top *Doctor Who* story for many fans: the SS-like Kaled élite are entirely credible in the context of centuries-long World War. And their fatally uncritical devotion to Davros as the brilliant engineer who might alone successfully win that war becomes equally believable. Well-drawn characters like Nyder add to the utterly true-to-life feel of this story. Similarly, one of the reasons *The Caves of Androzani* has at least an equal claim (or, as I see it, a better claim) to the prize of best *Doctor Who* story ever is because of the convincing nature of its two main contrasting villains, the passionate, revenge-driven Sharaz Jek, and the cold, calculating Traw Morgus, not to mention the more incidental but equally well-drawn gunrunner Stotz and his gang.

Motive – and especially credible motive – is such a key ingredient to the proper characterisation of villains. And a degree of subtlety (though not too confusing a degree!) adds enormously to this. That is why the entirely predictable and now mindlessly robotic Daleks of *Destiny of the Daleks* were such a disappointment, in contrast to the shockingly deceptive Daleks in *The Power of the Daleks*. The Daleks of the new series have regained something of their earlier, original, unpredictable and apparently undefeatable menace.

Religion is one motive which can elevate or destroy a society. This is true both in relation to its leaders (whether heroes, villains, or the complex mix much more common!) and its followers. Now it's *today's* religions, not the most 'primitive', that play a key rôle in the motivation of those ready to destroy the world; just as it's today's faiths that inspire those who would rebuild it (incidentally, I am not making a partisan religious point here, for different societies can point to the positive social impact of Martin Luther King and Gandhi, for example). So as the twenty-first century develops, the new series of *Doctor Who* will need to take that on board as a contributory element in its scripts.

Discussion: Why do you think religious commitment leads some people towards violent destruction, but inspires others to become leaders of peace and justice?

7

The Evil of the Daleks

Every so often, *Doctor Who* reinvents itself. In 1969, the Doctor was forced to regenerate, and was stripped by his Timelord judges of the ability to travel in his TARDIS, and so a series of adventures took place in the immediate future on Earth. Russell T. Davies has been keen to develop a dramatic new context for *Doctor Who*, a burgeoning back-story for the new series, with a catastrophic 'Time War' that saw the Doctor's planet and race destroyed, and many other races, too. But the episode *Dalek* made two major additions. In the Time War, the Daleks were the main protagonists, and the Doctor confidently tells us that the final phase of the Time War saw the end of his people and of all Daleks. However, the survival (just) of a solitary Dalek, even if very badly injured and captured by humans in the near future (2012), raises the first hint of uncertainty relating to this Time War.

In this brilliant story, author Robert Shearman successfully did the impossible, and made people feel sympathy for a Dalek! That apart, there are strong resonances with an earlier story, arguably the best Dalek story of the original series (though sadly only surviving in audio form, or reconstructed with TV still pictures), *The Power of the Daleks*, which similarly pictures a context of wounded, surviving Daleks (two, initially), who had been disarmed by humans. The Dalek once again responds animatedly to the Doctor, and unsuccessfully tries to kill him (its weapon is removed), speaking for the first time on recognising its old foe. By deception, it gains the power to take over, the Doctor's warnings being ignored at fatal cost, as a little army or two is easily killed.

So who are the Daleks?

In the world of *Doctor Who*, the answer to this question has varied over the years, each story subtly – or radically – modifying the response. The changes are as follows:

- *The Daleks* (1963–64): Indistinguishable from each other, they are radioactively mutated survivors of a neutron bomb war. Formerly the 'Dal' race, they are trapped in metal bodies and in a metal city, and are still determined to wipe out their ancient enemies on their planet, Skaro, the Thals – because they are different.
- *The Dalek Invasion of Earth* (1964): Now led by a Black Dalek, they are capable of conquering other planets, and have killed most humans, enslaving all the rest except for a handful of fugitives.
- *The Chase* (1965): They are brilliant, conquering time travel, in order to chase and kill the Doctor, who is now their chief enemy.
- *The Daleks' Masterplan* (1965–66): They are capable of

engineering an intergalactic takeover, and ruthless in despatching 'allies' after their usefulness ends.

- *The Power of the Daleks* (1966): They are long-dormant, revived creatures, who first speak when encountering the Doctor but fail to exterminate him (because disarmed). They are skilfully deceptive, gaining the power to revive a whole battery of themselves, to destroy a human colony.
- *The Evil of the Daleks* (1967): Now led by an Emperor Dalek (who commands Black Daleks and all others), they recognise and seek to reverse their failures, supposedly by forcing the Doctor to develop the charge that would mutate Daleks with a 'human factor', but actually to convert humans into Dalek-minded creatures.
- *Day of the Daleks* (1972), *Planet of the Daleks* and the preceding episode (1973), and *Death to the Daleks* (1974) add Ogron (sub-human) slaves, a readiness to work with the Master, and Dalek ingenuity in a planet where their weapons don't work.
- *Genesis of the Daleks* (1975) gives the most radical changes: They are now not just accidental radioactive mutations, but deliberate genetic mutations of their 'creator', the brilliant but deranged scientist Davros, and their predecessors are now not 'Dals' but the 'Kaled race', who provide the most explicit metaphor of the Daleks as space-age Nazis.
- *Destiny of the Daleks* (1979): Slaves of their own computer programmes, the Daleks need Davros's flair to defeat enemies.
- *Resurrection of the Daleks* (1984): The Daleks want to capture and control Davros, and Daleks loyal to the Black

Dalek and those engineered to follow Davros end up fighting each other.

- *Revelation of the Daleks* (1985): Davros' Daleks can use exterminated humans to reconstruct new Daleks;
- *Remembrance of the Daleks* (1988): Two Dalek races – one run by Davros (who calls himself Emperor), the other by the Black Dalek – fight each other (and humans and the Doctor) to obtain a powerful Timelord device.
- *Doctor Who: The Movie* (1996): They exterminated their one-time ally, the Master (or did they?). The biggest mistake to my mind in that film, which had many strengths and some major omissions, was not to start in the middle of the Dalek action, which is only narrated.

Now to all this we have two most recent developments:

- *Dalek* (2005): One Dalek survives the final Time War, awaits new Dalek orders, but starts to kill; however, its break-out is compromised by unintended mutation with what an earlier story called the 'human factor'.
- *Bad Wolf/The Parting of the Ways* (2005): They are led by an Emperor (like the 1967 Emperor, not Davros), who successfully avoided destruction in the Time War, and developed a new Dalek invasion army, but this development mutated Daleks into creatures ordering everyone not to blaspheme against the Emperor, who is now seen as their immortal god.

What all this (up to the new series) shows is two main Dalek story eras: before Davros and since. Since appearing, Davros stole most of the dialogue, and Daleks increasingly seemed vulnerable to human weapons, and not the invincible geniuses of the earliest stories. A different and interesting shift was from the old cause in nuclear physics to a new one in genetic biology – to which we return in Chapter 13.

The new series has reconceived the Daleks without Davros (whose invention of them is mentioned without naming him by the Ninth Doctor), in order to regain the earlier atmosphere of creatures that were virtually invincible, the ultimate war machine. The mistaken tease that they couldn't climb the stairs (*Destiny of the Daleks*) left viewers feeling it was easy to escape them – that they were no serious threat. So both new stories have decisively rectified that, with levitating Daleks, following the lead begun in *Remembrance of the Daleks*, but greatly improved. What's more, no baseball bat – or army of sub-machine-guns – can defeat the Daleks now: the most feared war machine in the galaxy begins to look and feel just that.

But who and what are the Daleks? What kind of threat, and what type of evil do they represent?

What is the evil of the Daleks?

If we take things beyond the simple idea that the Daleks are alien monsters who want to destroy and take over, and dig a little deeper, we will see that the Daleks are a metaphor for the Nazis. This implied dimension was made explicit in *Genesis of the Daleks* (1974).[1] There, we meet their precursor race –

---

[1] This uncontroversial point was well presented in the video *More Than Thirty Years in the TARDIS* (BBC, 1993).

now the Kaleds. This is an anagram (verbal mutation) of Daleks, as the organic unit in each travel machine is the 'final' post-radioactive mutation of the Kaled race, deliberately genetically mutated to become the ultimate fighting machine. As the Ninth Doctor explained in *Dalek*: 'It's a mutation. The Dalek race was genetically engineered. Every single emotion was removed – except hate.'

In *Genesis of the Daleks*, the Kaled uniforms look Nazi, their insignia are similar to the SS, and they click their heels together like Nazis. Davros' right-hand man, Nyder, comments, 'We must keep the Kaled race pure.'

If the Daleks are a metaphor for the Nazis, what does *Doctor Who* say about that evil, and how we should respond to it?

Years earlier, the first story pitched this issue as a debate between pacifism and resistance. Some of the rather pacifist Thals got killed for trying peaceful diplomacy. On the spectrum between a pacifist readiness to see all one's people killed rather than kill, and a gung-ho desire to kill others, the story implicitly applauds something like reluctant but determined resistance, as shown to the Thals by companion Ian Chesterton. Other stories follow the same pattern.

Genesis of the Daleks presents this in acute fashion. There is a moment when the Doctor has two leads in his hands. If he connected them, then, together with a bomb he had planted, the resulting explosion would have wiped out all Dalek life forms before they ever got started. But to the dismay of companions Harry and Sarah, he hesitates to commit genocide, even of these abominable hate-filled creatures:

Doctor: Have I that right?

Sarah: To destroy the Daleks? You can't doubt it!

Doctor: Well I do! You see, some things could be better with the Daleks. Many future worlds will become allies, just because of their fear of the Daleks. . . Do I have the right?

Even though much evil would be prevented by blowing up the tank of newly genetically created Daleks, the Doctor is reluctant to stop it, as he would be killing on a grand scale himself – perhaps becoming too uncomfortably close to the creatures themselves. The shock of *Dalek* is that the Ninth Doctor seems to have overstepped that mark, and the Dalek and Rose both recognise it. After one tirade, the Dalek comments, wryly: 'You would make a good Dalek', and at the end, as the Doctor angrily waves his advanced weapon at the now defenceless mutating Dalek creature, Rose protests that it is changing – and charges: 'What the hell are *you* changing into, Doctor?' Uncharacteristically, he is stopped in his tracks, nonplussed at the inescapable truth she revealed.

Actually, *Dalek* does not solve the problem of how to stop them. The Doctor ran out of ideas, and thought he had sacrificed Rose in the process of stalling the Dalek, when its mutation into a more human entity solved the problem. The same happened in *The Parting of the Ways*, where the Doctor resisted genocide, and would have died (along with humanity) but for Rose's extraordinary intervention.

In earlier stories, the Doctor often solved the problem simply by switching off the Daleks' power supply, or triggering their own weapons against them. In *The Evil of the Daleks*, the Doctor solved the problem in a different and far more acceptable way, humanising the Daleks – as also happened (by accident) in *Dalek*.

To what extent, when we face evil, can we sidestep the terrible challenges of doing evil to stop evil, and instead humanise and defeat our enemy not so much by killing him as by somehow turning him (or her) into our friend?

If we try to respond to this from the experience of the Bible, we find that the contexts of the Old and New Testaments are very different: the Old Testament engages in issues affecting the nation; the New Testament responds to issues impacting on clusters of small communities of believers scattered among many nations.

In the New Testament, the issue is of the largely powerless individuals facing the possibility of persecution. They hope to win over some by their model behaviour, but expect to get persecuted by others, despite it. Despite their vulnerability, they believe God is in charge and affects rulers, nations and international events (e.g. Mark 13). But with the exception of Paul attempting to convert King Agrippa (Acts 26), they do not expect to affect world affairs directly.

So as in *Dalek*, sometimes the problem cannot be solved, though our actions may on occasion lead to our persecutors being won over – by love.

But in the Old Testament, where the rulers of Israel are supposed to be faithful believers, the question of what to do in the face of major threats is more directly pressing. Now, the danger of facing mass extermination comes from outside, but there is a paradox: since God will keep such hostile forces at bay while his people still want him to be their God, the real danger comes from inside, as greedy, foolish and power-hungry leaders want to dispense with the God whose call for justice cramps their style. So mostly the Old Testament challenges the evil inside.

Of course, evil in pagan nations can be challenged and is (Amos 1–2), and pagan leaders can also be commended for honourable behaviour (Cyrus in Isaiah 44–45). But the dominant issue is summed up thus: the threat comes from outside, but the real danger is the evil within. We should expect to be attacked by hostile nations keen to expand their empires, but the real danger is of the evil of those who should be our help. When powerful insiders abuse their power, then external powers can *really* get destructive. Interestingly, this is actually a very common theme in *Doctor Who*, especially in Dalek stories, and leads us on to the 'secondary' villain.

The secondary evil: the opportunist collaborator

In *Dalek*, the Doctor's problems stem not only from the Dalek, but from Van Statten, who is a classic example of what we can call the 'secondary villain' in *Doctor Who*. This is where an alien danger is compounded by a human villain, motivated by greed, folly, or lust for power. And in *Dalek*, Van Statten's acquisitive greed and reckless contempt for the lives of those who might threaten his acquisitions fatally exacerbates the problem. The story *Dalek* illustrates this compounding of the problem: the evil and danger is centred on a Dalek, able to wipe out Salt Lake City and perhaps all humanity single-handedly; but it got so far partly because of

Van Statten. He follows a long line of opportunists, whose reprehensible behaviour shows that what it takes for evil to triumph is not simply (as in the old adage) for good men (or women) to do nothing. What really helps evil to get a hold, is if powerful people abuse their power for their own mis-guided, selfish purposes, by aligning themselves with evil because it suits them at the time. *Doctor Who* is full of cases of people in this mould. Solar system ruler Mavic Chen's betrayal in allying himself with Daleks because he thought he could increase his power is one vivid example (*The Daleks' Master Plan*). Van Statten's craze for acquiring alien personal possessions and power gives a much more paro-chial but highly believable example.

But if we go from *Doctor Who* to our world today, it is not at all hard to think of current and very controversial examples of this sort of behaviour; that is, pacts with very dangerous 'allies' – which I will simply raise as questions for readers and those engaged in discussion groups based on this to reflect on and discuss.

Discussion: When, in the 1980s, Saddam Hussein was sup-ported in order to destabilise Iran, and Osama bin Laden was supported, to undermine the Communists in Afghanistan, should those who armed or trained such people be accused of similar opportunism?
And should they have expected their actions to cause more problems than they solved?

8
Manipulating Myth Makers

Media magic

The Doctor makes two visits to Satellite Five, supposedly in a future golden age (the Fourth Great and Bountiful Human Empire during and soon after the year 200,000), but where things prove desperately wrong. In both cases, there is something so wrong with the media that the world is being destroyed without anyone realising it. *The Long Game* raises the spectre of propaganda, and *Bad Wolf* the corruptions of 'bread and circuses'.

The Long Game has many similarities to *The Macra Terror* – another early story only surviving in audio form, or reconstructed with stills (telesnaps) and video fragments. Here, too, the Doctor and companions arrive at a superficially very friendly, happy place, but which the Doctor soon recognises as a phoney, synthetic, engineered happiness. Once again, there is an industrious and unquestioning workforce (this time under an atmospheric, drug-induced mind-control), a society in the grip of almost unchallenged propaganda, for which the rare acts of dissent are spotted and eradicated, and which turns out to be dominated not by its alleged human controller, but by a hidden alien power, the Macra; they use the base and the controlled humans as agents for their own well-being, enslaving them. The Macra and Jagrafess are gigantic parasites.

So, beyond a typical yarn about monsters taking over the human race for their own benefit, *The Long Game* displays several other features, which press issues deeper. It highlights issues of propaganda and dissent. In a way, it is *Doctor Who*'s version of George Orwell's classic dystopian nightmare, *Nineteen Eighty-four*, and like that novel it can be seen as a satire on the propaganda-based totalitarian dictatorships of the old Communist world, and those that behave like them. There is also an implication that our own culture, which this 'happiness patrol' mimics, may be less free than we think. In that case, the monster becomes a metaphor for a conformity of our own making.

Myth makers, truth slayers

The Long Game pictures a world, a human era, where everyone believes the same – and everyone is wrong. More accurately, dissent is marginally possible, but ruthlessly eradicated. And unlike in *Nineteen Eighty-four* even the Winston Smiths, the people actually twisting the news, cannot possibly resist – because their bodies are dead.

One very positive issue this raises is the controversial one of truth. It is not a matter of opinion whether a human culture controlled by Jagrafess and one free of him are 'equally valid'. The story is very clear, and so is the Doctor:

Rose: So all the people on Earth are, like, slaves?

Editor: Well now, there's an interesting point. Is a slave a slave
   if he doesn't know he's enslaved?

Doctor: Yes!

Editor: Oh. I was hoping for a philosophical debate. Is that all
   I'm going to get – 'Yes'?

Doctor: Yes!

Clarity about truth, especially moral truth, has become
unpopular in many circles, and this story is a good antidote. If
truth, especially moral truth, is believed to be undiscoverable,
undefinable, or unreal, then the only alternative to guide society is the opinion poll approach: the majority of people
believe this to be true and that to be right, so they are.

But for 91 years everyone in the supposed Fourth Great and
Bountiful Human Empire has been believing a lie, a whole
stifling system of lies. All opinion polls could reveal 100 per
cent belief that the walls of level 500 are paved with gold, and
100 per cent support for the journalistic ethics of seeking pro-
motion to it, but they would all be wrong.

In a way, it is the classic comic children's fairy tale *The
Emperor's New Clothes*. And in *The Long Game*, the Doctor
plays the rôle of the little boy, through whom others see and
tell the truth.

History is replete with examples of great people who have
dared to say what 'conventional wisdom' denies, sometimes
convincing people at the time, sometimes failing and even
dying for their insights, but whose wisdom outlasts that of
their critics. In the Bible, Jeremiah prophesied – against most
voices – that God would not save Zion because Judah's

religion was so corrupt, and that they would be invaded, Jerusalem destroyed, and the leaders and much of the nation exiled for 70 years. And despite their derision at him, so it proved to be. In ancient Athens, Socrates was eventually executed because he refused to stop his form of questioning. But afterwards, his questioning spirit transformed Greek culture and the world. Galileo was forced to deny the truth he knew, that the Earth rotates around the Sun and not vice versa. But such abuse of power to save propaganda failed to stop people coming to accept that the Earth is not the centre of the universe. Luther challenged the abuse of indulgences as implying salvation could be bought, when it was God's act of grace that could never be earned by human deeds and gifts, but only trusted in and accepted by faith. He famously recognised that it seemed to be him against the whole world. But he had seen what the Bible said, and he could not twist it into a lie instead: 'Here I stand; I can no other!' He survived in hiding, and eventually many came to support him, much of the church enjoying a Reformation as a result; even the continuing Catholic lands experienced a different transformation of their own (the Counter-Reformation), as the medieval corrupt church could not endure. Thomas Helwys, the first Baptist in England, declared his belief in print that the government should permit all law-abiding religions to be able to flourish, that there should be complete religious freedom, not just for dissenters, but for Catholics, Jews and Muslims – and got sent to the Tower of London. But now his view is a commonplace in this land and across the globe. And so we could continue with many other examples.

In the world of the Soviet Union and other Communist

states, there was often a heavy price to pay for dissent. But the dissenters were proved right. In 1969, when dissident Andrei Amalrik wrote *Will the Soviet Union Survive until 1984?*, he questioned whether Soviet society, unchanged, could survive for many more years. He was sent to the Gulag, and the authorities assumed their actions could sustain the lie. But Amalrik was right. The cracks were appearing, and eventually led to the collapse of Communism from 1989 to 1991.

There is sometimes a cost for telling the truth, especially an unpopular truth, one that is unpopular with those who hold power and who try to keep hold of it brutally, like Jagrafess. However, in the end, brutality can't stop the truth from creeping – or exploding – out.

All this reminds us that the truth, whether scientific, moral or spiritual, is not the combined beliefs of the current majority. So we should not allow mockery to cajole us out of unconventional viewpoints, as if deviating from current majority beliefs was automatically absurd. Indeed, so many of the most major scientific, cultural, moral and spiritual achievements have been won against the previous consensus, that this is now the way we see how science itself advances. T.S. Kuhn's *The Structure of Scientific Revolutions* showed how when science makes its major advances, there is something of a 'paradigm shift' from the previous model of understanding to the new one. The advance of course is not haphazard: a new theory emerges which better explains more factors than the one it replaces.[1]

---

[1] T. S. Kuhn: *The Structure of Scientific Revolutions* (University of Chicago Press, 1962; 2nd enlarged edn, 1970). Of course this issue is more complex. The phrase I used, 'better explains', implies a subjective

But this sort of progress is not only true in relation to science, but also to moral and spiritual advances. As philosopher Renford Bambrough once put it: 'Galileo was right when he contradicted the Cardinals: and so was Wilberforce when he rebuked the slave-owners.'[2]

There are two sides to this equation in *The Long Game*: not only was it right for brilliant but loyal journalist Cathica to break free from majority opinion and fight for the truth instead; also society had gone dangerously wrong with its manipulated uniformity. Group mentalities can foster conspiracies of evil. Those who have studied the psychology of suicide bombers find not deranged or suicidal members of the oppressed poor, but ordinary people (usually young and male) sympathetic to a cause, who are encouraged into small units, sharing a joint commitment to their goal – which makes it hard to back out.[3] No doubt the collective evil of the Nazis demonstrates this on the larger scale. Of course, the collective failures of societies in *The Macra Terror* and *The Long Game* are provoked by alien manipulation. But the monsters are a picture of the monstrous evil that can happen when a collective consensus to cut out our critical responses takes place.

---

dimension, and as Kuhn shows, 'paradigm debates always involve the question: Which problems is it more significant to have solved?' – *ibid.*, p. 110.

[2] Renford Bambrough: 'A Proof of the Objectivity of Morals' in Robert L. Cunningham (ed.): *Situationism and the New Morality* (Appleton-Century-Crofts, 1970), p. 110.

[3] See for example Michael Bond, 'The Ordinary Bombers' in *New Scientist* (23 July 2005), p. 18.

Discussion: If all our friends take a different point of view from us, how easy is it to stand up for what we believe?

Big brother

The episode *Bad Wolf* returned us to Satellite Five. But this time, the 'Big Brother' encountered was not George Orwell's original concept, but the reality TV show, or a distorted version of it, supposedly still running in 198,000 years' time! Those fans who like their *Doctor Who* to veer towards 'hard' science fiction will no doubt recoil at the deliberate anachronisms of *Bad Wolf* with today's TV surviving in only slightly modified form for 200 millennia. This however is *Doctor Who* at its fantasy end, and the scriptwriters were having fun by modifying Anne Robinson of *The Weakest Link*, with only a small number of adjustments, into Anne Droid the death-ray-delivering game-show host, and the other shows. This surreal game-show context is not merely absurd for its own sake, but uses this exaggerated form to highlight the idea of today's culture providing dangerously escapist 'bread and circuses'.

Bread and circuses

The Roman satirist Juvenal (AD 55–127) commented that while people used to hanker after military commands and promotions, now they just long for 'bread and circuses'. In other words, a people sated with enough food and escapist entertainment will drop their ambitions, not to mention critical faculties, and settle for mediocrity and stupor.

Star Trek's take on this quotation was a parallel Earth where Rome never fell, with gladiatorial contests to the death on TV, but challenged by a religious group parallel to Christians in the name of the Son, and the brotherhood of man.

The Third Doctor also referred to Juvenal's celebrated comment in *The Paradise of Death* (an early audio story), quoting it in Latin, as the Brigadier begins to react to that planet's culture, which provides 'experienced reality' entertainment of executions by hunting and killing people:

Brigadier: Gladiators, by Jiminy!
Doctor: To keep the plebs quiet. The Romans had a word for it, or rather three words: '*panem et circenses*' – 'bread and circuses'. It worked then. It works now.

The Long Game showed up how TV can be used as propaganda. But *Bad Wolf* pursues the 'bread and circuses' issue – how TV (or other compulsive entertainment) can easily distract populations from worthwhile purpose, ambition, or even from questioning. In this case, it presumably suited the Daleks to allow the vicious but compulsive TV-addicted culture to dominate, and so keep the population distracted from asking serious questions (like: 'What's happening on our interplanetary doorstep?'), and use the 'evictions' to build up their workforce. Executions as TV entertainment, combined with Daleks generated from exterminated humans, recollect the Sixth Doctor stories *Vengeance on Varos* and *Revelation of the Daleks*.

To what extent is our culture guilty of merely providing full stomachs and compulsive entertainment? And to what extent is it fair to say that this is done at the expense of true culture?

There is no doubt that a close examination of these questions in relation to our experience of life in Western culture triggers a none-too-comfortable response. Our culture has had unparalleled success in providing 'bread' for its own people. However, as the starvation of many continues, especially in Africa, this glut has been achieved in a divisive way. Much talk of 'free trade' has obscured protectionism, and so free trade will not be free until it is fair – i.e. equally free, not protected to secure European and American market domination of Africa, for example.

As for the 'circuses', it is of course possible that TV, as well as other media, can be a profound force for good. In the UK, in 1965, the compelling drama *Cathy Come Home* was so brilliantly written and challenging that it provoked the setting up of Shelter, the charity for the homeless, and radically changed attitudes. But too often media of all sorts (those who write for them, that is) lose this cutting edge, and simply write for entertainment and profit. And then Juvenal's slur applies.

Of course, the writers can justifiably retort that they can only write what stands a chance of being performed, and that means what viewers will watch. So if we want TV – including *Doctor Who* – to become stimulating and challenging, really worth watching and even inspiring, then we must demand that and support it. There will be plenty of writers keen to write for brave, innovative, stimulating and challenging TV, determined to aim at inspiration and greatness, if only there will be those equally keen to be stimulated.

Some may wonder what this has to do with Christianity.

Everything! For this is about the rôle we play in our culture. Christian faith is not about creating or hiding in some cultural ghetto, nor is it about imposing that ghetto on everybody else. It is about being so inspired and inspiring through our vision that it becomes positively contagious, so that the culture as a whole becomes immeasurably enriched.

Back in the seventeenth century, Blaise Pascal in his brilliant *Pensées* made one of his provocative observations which is pertinent here: 'People despise Christian faith [*la religion*]. They hate it and are afraid it may be true. The solution for this is to show them, first of all, that it is not unreasonable, that it is worthy of reverence and respect. Then show that it is winsome, making good men desire that it were true. Then show them that it really is true. It is worthy of reverence because it really understands the human condition. It is also attractive because it promises true goodness.'[4] The question is, is the expression of our Christian vision 'winsome'?

Discussions: What cultural differences can and should we be aiming to make, in our own local context, and further afield?

Is *Doctor Who* itself just 'bread and circuses', and could it play a more culturally challenging rôle for its viewers?

---

[4] Blaise Pascal: *Pensées* (incomplete before his death, 1662, first published in French, 1669–70), translated; edited by James Houston in *The Mind on Fire* (Hodder & Stoughton, 1991), #187–12, p. 52. In traditional editions following Léon Brunschvig, this comes in Section III, 'On the Necessity of the Wager'.

9

Time Travelling Temptations

There is a major sub-plot in *The Long Game*, which makes this story new in *Doctor Who*, and which is revealed by Russell T. Davies's original story outline title, *The Companion Who Couldn't*.

Unlike most examples of the triumph (or near triumph) of evil, which home in on monsters of evil and their usually willing collaborators, this story illustrates the downfall of a potential hero who failed. Evil nearly triumphs because an ordinary person – not a megalomaniac – couldn't resist temptation. So this side of the story is a study in temptation and how we fall to it – and what the consequences are, where personal responsibilities lie and where excuses fail.

The time meddler

What Adam in *The Long Game* is guilty of is succumbing in a big way to the temptation to steal knowledge. Now as it happens, after the temptations of the megalomaniac, this is probably the next most common temptation in *Doctor Who*, and intriguingly, too, is the primal sin of Adam, not to mention Eve, in the Garden of Eden. Do not steal the fruit of the tree of knowledge! And neither Adam can resist that temptation.

But this turns out to be a recurring issue, and it's not only villains who fall. The Doctor himself was after all on the run from the Time Lords in his original form, and first regeneration, partly because he wanted to steal – acquire – knowledge that the Time Lords deemed too dangerous, because (they believed) interaction with all the life-forms would inevitably disrupt the true course of history. We can see this in the earliest stories quite clearly. What's more, the Doctor deceived his companions about a fault in the mercury component of the fluid links of the TARDIS, ultimately putting the ship and them all in danger, because he was so keen to see (and so to know about) the 'dead' city from the inside (in *The Daleks*).

Earlier companions are not beyond this temptation either: Zoe and Adric want to be stowaways on board the TARDIS because they want to steal a ride and so have the experience – the knowledge – of other times and places.

But Adam crosses a further line. He would have this knowledge and abuse it in order to gain from it, changing the course of history to suit his selfish ends. He may not realise that he is a time meddler, but he is corrupting Earth's future simply to gain an unfair advantage. He is cheating in the exam of life.

We will return to the issues of the temptation to abuse time travel itself later. But what about temptation in general? As for the controversial dimensions of the story of the Garden of Eden, I will take it as read that among readers, both non-Christian and Christian, there will be different attitudes to it. Some will take the story straight, almost as a journalist's report of what actually happened literally; some will also accept it as broadly true, but take it as some kind of a poetic but true picture of a fall of mankind that happened; others will see it as an old fable with some insight into the human condition; others will dismiss it or ignore it entirely. Discussing all that any further takes us well beyond our remit in this book! But the least controversial observation is noting the way this account illustrates the reality of temptation and how it operates, the way it can trip basically good people up, in a way that can lead to bad and even dreadful results.

Peter Purves, the one time *Blue Peter* presenter who earlier played companion Steven Taylor (1965–66), once suggested that he could have been persuaded to return as Steven, some years after he had been left to rebuild the society of *The Savages* (1966). But he imagined Steven abusing the powerful situation he had been left in. Purves suggested Steven might find it difficult to avoid the temptations of using his advanced skills to his advantage, and 'have become a fascist dictator fairly quickly and had millions of concubines.'[1] 'Power tends to corrupt; absolute power corrupts absolutely' in Lord Acton's memorable dictum. To help prevent our societies from succumbing to this temptation, there is a strong argument to try to ensure that society sees the dispersal of power rather than the concentration of it.

Towards the end of *The Long Game*, when Adam faces the Doctor's wrath, he tries to turn it aside with a string of excuses

---

[1] Peter Purves in conversation with Steve Lyons and Chris Howarth in 'King of the Savages', *Doctor Who Magazine #220* (December 1994), p. 8; that he would be ready to play Steven for a story set in that situation, *ibid.*, p. 9.

and explanations: 'I'm alright now. Much better. I've got my key. . . Look, it all worked out for the best, didn't it? What? You know it's not actually my fault because you were in charge. . .' All these weasel words show that he thinks that his disclosed, reprehensible behaviour didn't *really* matter, that it was the Doctor's fault anyway, for leaving him to his own devices (a denial of personal responsibility). And to cap it all, when the Doctor has escorted him home, the Doctor gives him one last chance not to cheat: 'Is there anything *else* you want to tell me?' He lamely replies, 'No. Erm. What do you mean?' The Doctor destroys the stored data, one second of which would have disrupted the fabric of history.

Now Adam's comments are not completely without justification. The Doctor leaves the disorientated young boffin in a place where it's just too easy to help himself to the research 'break' to end them all, and he's surprised that Adam falls? But the Doctor is right. Adam is not a child. He is responsible for his own choices. And he is guilty of attempting to steal not merely an unfair advantage, but the whole destiny of the human race for himself.

There are major responsibilities in entering the TARDIS, a world where the experiences gained could be used to benefit, corrupt or even destroy humanity. The challenge was too great for Adam. But could Rose Tyler also be susceptible to this temptation? Not the exact form that proved Adam's undoing, the temptation to acquire unique knowledge for personal gain, but one more suited to her own vulnerability, the temptations rooted in the pain and longings of a child whose father died in her infancy? That is a central theme of *Father's Day*.

Risk

The Ninth Doctor is something of a risk-taker – he shares that with earlier Doctors. But he takes risks with his companions, too. Whatever gap in time there is between the three stories (and little is implied) in *Father's Day*, it is not long since the Doctor thought he had risked and lost Rose's life to stall a Dalek on the loose, and even less time since he allowed Adam to go on the loose in AD 200,000 – a risk which backfired badly. And yet here he is, allowing Rose to go back in time to be present at the very moment her father got run over and killed, as no one was with him when he died. And the story tells of her first bottling it, too shocked to act in time, and then, when the Doctor takes an even bigger risk, returning to the same point in time, hiding behind their concurrent selves, she does not simply move to hold the dying man's hand, but rushes out early enough to prevent the accident, save his life – and change history.

Time paradoxes

The idea of travelling in time is a great science fantasy, which stimulates the imagination, and of course underlies the whole of *Doctor Who*. However, all programmes that engage in the idea of time travel as a reality, if they permit this to happen with any frequency in their writings, face major paradoxical problems. There's no problem if time travel is only undertaken once, or in very restricted contexts, like H.G. Wells' original novel *The Time Machine*, or even the TV series *Babylon 5*. But *Star Trek* and, even more, *Doctor Who* hit the problem of time paradoxes – and have solved them in very different ways.

Star Trek never goes back into time before the present – except to situations where time meddling results in Hitler winning World War II – a recurring favourite. In such stories, it pictures time travel as capable of changing history every time. The crew must go back themselves and stop the reversal happening.

Doctor Who is very different. Many of its stories take its crew into the past, and instead there is a suggestion that time is governed by laws that make it hard, unwise or impossible to change history.

However, there is a credibility problem with the way this works out which has led to a gradual change in the way intervention in history is pictured. The paradox is this: when the Doctor and companions enter our past, they are told they cannot and must not affect the course of history; but when they enter our future they change it every time. They can't stop Hitler or Robespierre but can stop Davros and Cassandra. As we shall see, Rose throws this accusation of inconsistency at the Doctor.

Of course the reason why script editors invented such laws of time is clear enough. After the Doctor has saved the Thals on Skaro from the Daleks, why can't he save people from Robespierre's *Reign of Terror*?

The equivalent to *Father's Day* in the original series setting up the answers to the paradoxes of time was *The Aztecs*. The locals, seeing companion Barbara with jewellery from a sealed tomb, believe her to be a reincarnation of Yetaxa. Barbara, a history teacher, knows the period well, and tries to exploit her position to persuade the leader to end human sacrifice, but the Doctor advises her that her attempt is both foolish and impossible – and the outcome proves him right.

The Massacre of St Bartholomew's Eve says the same – with one tiny difference: the Doctor may not flaunt the flow of history, but can get away with tweaking it a bit, arguably guiding a servant girl to safety. In the story, the difference is not enough for Steven Taylor to notice. He quits the TARDIS in disgust at the Doctor's reluctance to meddle enough to save Anne Chaplet, only to return and find Dodo, her supposed descendant, accidentally on board. As commentator John Peel noted: 'I have problems with the whole Anne [Chaplet] issue. The Doctor, claiming he can't change history, leaves her to (possibly) die. But he has no qualms about taking along Dodo later in the episode! (And how contrived is it that she just happens to be Anne's great-great whatever?) You can tell Donald Tosh wrote that bit!'[2]

Later, the Second Doctor commented: 'I'm not exactly breaking the laws of time, but I am bending them a little.' And that's as far as it went.

The effect of this was to see the Doctor adopting near fatalism when in human history, but dramatically changing the future without hesitation – saving the Earth in c.2167 in *The Dalek Invasion of Earth*, for example.

Later, in *Day of the Daleks*, the Third Doctor presented

---

[2] John Peel, comment on the *Loose Cannon* Reconstruction of *The Massacre of St Bartholomew's Eve*, quoted on their website: www.recons.com/recons/lc16.htm Incidentally, the TV story and John Lucarotti's original script, and the novelisation he wrote based on that script, are radically different. The effect at this point in the script is that Lucarotti's Doctor does actually interfere a little.

technobabble (the 'Blinovitch Limitation Effect') to argue laws of time – to explain to companion Jo that the guerrillas couldn't go back in time to five minutes earlier to prevent the Daleks taking over, because they would meet themselves, creating a time paradox, the exact effects of which are un-explained in that story.

How this time paradox works was explored in *Mawdryn Undead*, with the Brigadier suffering severe loss of memory between the two times when he met himself as a result. Rose was spared that ordeal by the scriptwriters!

But over the years two major developments have changed the way this time paradox is seen. First, purely historical stories were more or less replaced by stories where alien mon-sters invaded our past – Daleks, for example, in *The Evil of the Daleks*, invading Victorian England for their purposes. So the Doctor *can* now enter our past and save everyone from vil-lains, but the villains will be time-meddling Sontarans for example, or the Master (in *The King's Demons*), rather than historical human villains.

The other change has been in the development of the idea of the time monsters called 'Reapers' we see in *Father's Day*. Though there are differences, I am reminded of the Vortisaurs in *Storm Warning* (a *Doctor Who – Big Finish* audio story with the Eighth Doctor set in the R101 disaster of 1930). They, too, are creatures of the time–space vortex – 'Vultures!' the Doctor calls them. This idea of monsters in time began in *The Time Monster* (1972), with Chronovores, monsters that can devour time and with it the lives of those in that time. The mightiest is Kronos, a creature with cosmic powers of time, which the Master wanted to exploit.

But *Father's Day* – apart from these Reapers – was in many ways a purely historical story. And, like *The Aztecs*, it establishes early for viewers the limits to the Doctor's powers. He can't go into the past and simply prevent the holocaust, it appears. (However, he will still go into the future and stop Dalek holocausts!)

It is this inconsistency Rose challenges, when the Doctor attacks her as 'another stupid ape' for reckless time meddling in saving her father's life:

Rose: So it's OK when *you* go to other times and *you* save people's lives, but not when it's me saving my dad?

Doctor: I know what I'm doing; you don't! Two sets of us there made that a vulnerable point.

Rose: But he's alive. . .

Doctor: My entire planet died, my whole *family*; do you think it never occurred to *me* to go back and save them?

This picture of time is rather less absolute and fixed than the First Doctor painted from *The Aztecs* onwards. But it still implies that we can't go back to the past and save our dads – even if we have a TARDIS.

Now a lot of this is in a way a bit arcane – only relevant if you want to imagine yourself into the world of TARDIS time travel and all its puzzles. But the questions raised are more relevant than that. For the twists and turns of time travel paradoxes raise in an acute fashion the whole question of fate or destiny versus free will. They also raise the questions of causality, of the course of history and what forces (if any) can or should change it.

Is time fixed? Is history set on a fixed course? Such questions are often also tied up with the related issues of determinism, the idea that our actions are determined by forces we ourselves do not control.

Many thinkers have come to support various versions of fatalism and/or determinism. Karl Marx saw history as an inevitable struggle between *economic* forces that was bound to lead in the end to the final battle between exploiting managers (the bourgeoisie) and exploited workers (the proletariat). Though individuals could of course opt to assist or resist that cause, its victory was inevitable.

Sigmund Freud presented the view that psychological experiences determined a person's development, though he also wanted to say that it made a difference whether a person underwent psychoanalysis or not. Freud also wanted to assert that religion was induced by psychological factors. However, the assertion that all people's religious views are determined by their psychological experiences defeats itself, as that view parallels the gloriously illogical statement: 'All generalisations are false – including this one!'

Émile Durkheim, the founder of sociology, preferred to argue that social factors determined behaviour. And of course we could point to those theological systems that suggest that our ultimate destiny is fixed by God. This has been a major fault-line in Christian debate, with some like Augustine, Luther and Calvin pressing the argument towards the pole of our destiny (in heaven or hell) being fixed by God before time, and others like Wesley the opposite pole, that free response to the gospel is possible, desirable and no illusion.

This is such a big issue that even the Doctor is not

completely sure. There is one scene in *Inferno* where the Third Doctor muses, excitedly, 'So free will is not an illusion!' However, as we have seen, in many stories it *is* an illusion. So in *Earthshock*, it seems that Adric's freighter 'was always' going to wipe out the dinosaurs, implying that he is predestined to crash, and all the earlier actions are fated.

In the journey of life, is our course more like a journey on a tram (completely fixed, unchangeable), a trolleybus (a fixed journey, though we can sway a bit to the left or right), a bus (where the route is predictable, but could in principle change), or a car, with us as the drivers (where the choice of route is ours)?

In practice, both extremes, though tidier systematically, hit insurmountable problems. The idea that we are the masters of our own destiny, though reinforced by many political statements about 'freedom', and obviously a widespread human desire, is clearly untrue to experience. It is of course true that factors other than our personal choices will affect history and our place in it. But the opposite extreme of presuming our lives purely fixed by other factors is also untrue to our experience. Our choices may not make all the difference to everything, but they make some differences to some things.

And in the theological sphere, the difficulties of the poles are just as clear. Ignore one pole and God seems to control us so much that we have no personal responsibility; ignore the opposite pole and God seems powerless in history, not sovereign Lord. The Bible does not pursue either pole exclusively, but sees God as Lord of history and our destiny, while affirming that our choices are real and make a difference. To use the picture above, that means we are nearer to the bus or trolleybus than the car or tram.

Similarly, Shakespeare's much-quoted comment, 'There's a divinity that shapes our ends, rough-hew them how we will' is closer to the 'trolleybus' picture.[3]

The theological concept to express this balance between predestination and personal responsibility biblically is providence. God guides our lives, and we can co-operate with that guidance. He is in charge of history, but we are players in history, and can rebel, or trust him.

Discussion: If, like Pete Tyler, I act heroically to save someone's life, is that my good act, or am I fated to do that by my genes, upbringing or social context, or indeed by God?
And if, like Cassandra, I act callously to harm or kill, am I also fated by outside forces, or even God, or am I freely acting, and showing evil?
Am I responsible – or is free will an illusion?

---

[3] William Shakespeare: *Hamlet V*, ii.

10

The Doctor in the Moral Maze

At the start, we saw that *Doctor Who* is more than an adventure series with our heroes facing monstrous evil, more also than the high octane emotional drama it now offers in Russell T. Davies' hands; it is also a contemporary morality tale. The battle is with evil, in which the Doctor does not simply defeat evil militarily but also morally; he avoids capitulating to the morality of his villainous foes.

But the Doctor is not alone, and sometimes his morality and that of his companions collides. As we saw earlier, Sarah Jane challenged the Doctor's timidity in not wiping out the Daleks. But this was most obvious in the classic series with the Brigadier, who for example was happy to blow up the Silurians with whom the Doctor still wanted to create a *modus vivendi*. His characteristic, gung-ho 'Five rounds, rapid!' order (in *The Daemons*) clearly conflicts with the Doctor's more thoughtful and diplomatic approach. And if Jack Harkness meets up with the Doctor often enough, we can expect a similar tension.

But at the heart of the new series in the opening seasons lies the relationship between the Doctor and Rose. And this certainly includes a strong moral tension, as shown in his angry rejection of her as 'another stupid ape' when she is elated at having just saved her father's life. She's in the immediate moral context (I had the opportunity to save his life, so it's right that I did), while he is operating at the grand level of preventing disruptions to space and time, to save the lives of many from the devastating dangers created by the 'Reapers'. But perhaps this moral tension between Rose's local, human perspective and the Doctor's trans-local, alien outlook is most clearly illustrated by the Doctor's sharp retort to Rose's revulsion at the Doctor's acceptance of Gelth proposals in *The Unquiet Dead* to inhabit corpses:

Rose: You can't let them run around in the dead people!

Doctor: Why not? It's like recycling.

Rose: Seriously, though, you can't. . .

Doctor: Seriously, though, I can.

Rose: But it's just wrong. Those bodies were living people. We should respect them in death.

Doctor: Do you carry a donor card?

Rose: It's different.

Doctor: It *is* different. It's a different morality. Get used to it or go home!

The implications for the Doctor's ethical stance implied here are very interesting. The 'get used to it' jibe clearly implies he *has* got used to it. He has been around the universe a lot, and has got used to thousands of different ways of doing things. He is not going to be tied down to the provincial morality and cultural prejudice of Earth, or Gallifrey. So he will be at home in vastly different cultures – and moralities. This has always been a feature in *Doctor Who* to some extent. The First Doctor revelled in adapting to his culture, whether that meant he had to manoeuvre his way through the complexities of court intrigue before Richard the Lion-Heart, kowtow to Kublai Khan, or pretend to be a lyre player before Nero.

The Doctor clearly has his own ethical code – and Rose finds it disturbing more than once. We start with that classic moral dilemma – whether it is ever right to kill – as illustrated by the Doctor's action in causing the death of the scheming and murderous Cassandra in *The End of the World*. Rose expresses our shock. But the Doctor's actions and possible justifications raise one of the biggest ethical debates, and enable us to examine not only the Doctor's possible motives and justification, but ours, too. After that, we turn to *Boom Town*, which recapitulates the moral issues arising from *The End of the World*, in the form of local versus universal justice: should terrorists, like the Slitheen disguised as Margaret Blaine, be deported to planets where they will face grotesque torture and execution? That is what she can expect on her return home, so that is the 'justice' the Doctor would deliver her into. This raises the question of whether we should respect a multicultural patchwork of varied, local moralities, or aim at universal forms of justice.

And then we can compare the Doctor's alien morality with ethical difficulties for humans. For we have already seen the almost fatal temptations for Adam and the different – but equally nearly lethal – problems for Rose. But it is the answer of Rose's dad, Pete Tyler, to the moral maze that solves that otherwise intractable dilemma. His unexpected action discloses a better way. And finally we return to the slippery Slitheen – and the TARDIS' solution to the moral challenge – and the implications of that.

Is murder ever justified?

The End of the World raises this classic question with devastating force. Rose is shocked – and so are we. The Doctor teleports Cassandra, the last human (and murderer) back from her hideout, knowing she will quickly die without her moisturising attendants. When Rose challenges him for not saving her, and provoking her death, he simply shrugs it off: 'Everything has its time.'

But how can and do we judge such fundamental ethical questions? Today, whether we realise it or not, the debate is shaped by a secularist perspective. Since about 1750, the ruling classes in Europe and its colonies have increasingly ruled religious beliefs out of politics and ethics. But actually, the secular alternative is unresolved.

1. In the black and white corner is the absolutist. The attempt was made to devise morality based on reason. In the 1780s, philosopher Immanuel Kant thought he had discovered the solution to provable, rational ethics: only behaviour you can *always* want to pursue would be valid. Universalising: you couldn't want everyone *always* to lie, or murder, and so on, but you could want everyone always to tell the truth, save life, and the rest.[1] But Kant's solution failed: these

---

[1] Immanuel Kant: *Groundwork of the Metaphysic of Morals* (1785) – Eng. tr. and commentary in H. J. Paton: *The Moral Law* (Hutchinson: 1948, and frequently reprinted).

'absolutes' can't all be absolute, because sometimes they clash, inescapably.

The classic example is the problem of answering a murderer who asks if you know where a person he wants to murder is hiding. Do you mislead him, lie, but save the man's life, or tell the truth, so consigning the victim to death? Truth and saving life are both absolute, but they clash.

2. In the grey corner is the pragmatist. We know this as utilitarianism, refined by John Stuart Mill, but simplest with Jeremy Bentham's principle (also first expressed in the 1780s), that good behaviour entails ensuring 'the greatest happiness of the greatest number.'[2] Situation Ethics was a vaguely Christian echo of this in the 1960s, in which Joseph Fletcher replaced Bentham's philosophical 'greatest happiness' with the Christian-sounding demand for 'agape, i.e., Christian love'.[3] Both solve the problem of competing values by having only one: Do what promotes happiness (or love)! The reason this fails is a bit more complex. One problem is that it doesn't allow us to say simply, 'Murder is wrong!' Instead, it says, 'Murder is sometimes right, depending on whether, overall, it promotes happiness or not.' We recoil at being left with just a calculation of 'loving consequences'.

Secondly, Bentham and Fletcher fail in reducing everything to one principle. The greatest happiness (or most loving thing)

---

[2] Jeremy Bentham: *An Introduction to the Principles of Morals and Legislation* (1789), partly reproduced in John Stuart Mill: *Utilitarianism - including other essays* by him, and by Bentham and Austen (ed. Mary Warnock) (Fontana, 1962). See esp. note 4 on pp. 36–38 (Bentham's footnote of 1822), and p. 33, and note 1.

[3] Joseph Fletcher: *Situation Ethics* (SCM 1966).

and the greatest number already give us two variables. Which is better?

An example: If I decide to give away £10,000, which is better, to give it all to one person (maximising benefit for that person), or to give one penny to a million different people? Or is one of the thousands of compromise possibilities between those extremes better? The example also reveals a third, hidden variable: we might say that we should give more to those in greater need. In real life this would guide our giving to charity. But this gives rise to a third conflicting variable: 'the greatest good to the greatest number in the greatest need'. Bearing in mind all the needs of the six billion humans, not to mention animals, that leaves trillions of ethical possibilities for this gift. This 'simple' principle does not remove all conflicting variables. Neither pole works. The question is unresolved.

3. In the middle we have the part-time absolutist. Actually, what our Western secular-dominated societies have defaulted to is an awkward, confused mishmash between these two poles. Some of our law and politics is absolutist: all our talk of 'inalienable human rights', the right to life and so on. Such talk persuades many (especially in Europe) that the State should not take life in the form of capital punishment, for example. But some modern law and politics is pragmatist. For example, one argument by those promoting abortion law reform in Britain in 1967 was that legalising abortion would help society avoid the worst situations of backstreet abortions, and so on. This argument was clearly based on weighing various benefits, and promoting that which it expected to cause the greater overall happiness.

Into this context, first of all, we can place the Doctor's

awkward behaviour. The Ninth Doctor seems to be quick to engage in 'rough justice', even quicker than the Sixth. Indeed, his behaviour is far removed from that of previous Doctors. Even the somewhat self-seeking First Doctor clearly rejected such behaviour in *The Dalek Invasion of Earth*: 'No, Tyler, no! I never take life. Only when my own is immediately threatened.'

With Cassandra, the Ninth Doctor seems to be acting not on the basis of beliefs in human rights – the right to a fair trial and so on. Instead, he delivers summary execution. He might argue it on utilitarian lines: Cassandra might escape and then kill others, so we've got to ensure she dies before she does it again, and so on. And such reasoning might hide other unacknowledged motives: how *dare* she kill creatures like Jabe (a sentient, tree-based life-form, who died helping the Doctor save everyone from Cassandra's attack) and then taunt us? His comment, 'everything has its time' is a kind of (weak) justification: her continued existence was so expensive that it required other people to suffer to enable her to raise the cash to keep herself alive. The Doctor judges that she is a dangerous parasite who must die that others may live.

The 'human rights' absolutist in us recoils at his behaviour. The 'utilitarian' in us recognises the awkwardness of difficult judgements, such as when Romanians killed their overthrown dictator Ceausescu in 1989, for fear he might somehow escape, regain power and kill all opponents; or when police killed a (wrongly) suspected suicide bomber in 2005.

4. And in the Christian corner? Are Christians simply obliged to imitate the same tensions, but just use religious words for the same tough choices, or does the revelation in

the Bible ensure a different response? And if it does, how can Christians promote as right an ethical policy based on principles the unbeliever can't accept or even access?

It's true that the Christian take on these issues often looks like the same debate couched in religious language. Some sound absolutist, saying that murder, theft and false witness for example are wrong, but base this not on reason but on the Ten Commandments. Others, especially at the more liberal end of the spectrum, sound pragmatist, opting for situation ethics based on loving your neighbour as the overriding principle.

However, this misses the key dimension. Christian ethics is not the same (or even different) abstract principles obtained by different means; it is a different context. The key Christian insight is that we should love God and our neighbour because God first loved us. This is centre stage in the New Testament, of course: Jesus died on the cross to express God's love for us, and to motivate our love for God and for our neighbour. But it is also there, less prominently, in the Old Testament, where the love of God for his people is expressed in saving them from slavery in Egypt before calling them to the distinctive life based on the Ten Commandments. Christian values are not abstract principles, but are expressed in the context of a relationship with God. They express the calling to live life in response to God.

What does this mean for the very specific context of the Doctor and Cassandra? Jesus called us to love our enemies (Matthew 5:44). Not the easiest of his words to put into practice, and certainly not one that could ever be the official law of any land. But it arises from this relationship context: if we live life on the basis of our relationship with God more consistently, then we see that our enemies are also loved by God. They may be undeserving of that love, perhaps even more undeserving of it than we are! But God loves our enemies, and Christ died for them. So how can we act so that they might experience the love of God? We need to uncover our unworthy motives, like revenge. We will not get it right. But we seek to get it more nearly right.

Meanwhile, can the rightness of this Christian 'take' on these ethical problems be proved as right to the secularist? No. Not in some knock-down proof that obliges the secularist to adopt these values or the faith they express. Instead, the Christian life, including its ethical dimension, can and should validate itself not in proving its worth mathematically, but in inspiring the person affected, because love always has an effect. But that effect can also be resisted.

Afterthought: It's hard enough to love your enemy who's only being spiteful to you, let alone if she murders your friends. . .

Discussion: Could the Doctor's action in killing Cassandra ever be justified?

The brink of disaster

In a multicultural – or intergalactic – society, how should we handle conflicting ethical outlooks? Should the Doctor respect all local ethics and customs? Or try to discover and live by a universal moral code? As we have just seen, our culture is torn, as the Doctor is torn. And this is illustrated dramatically in the story *Boom Town*. After the failure of the Slitheen attempt to wipe out the human race with nuclear weapons, and make a 'killing' on the financial rewards of a radiated planet, Blon Fel Fotch Passameer-Day Slitheen ('Margaret Blaine') had escaped and, posing as mayor of Cardiff, aims to repeat the exercise, until captured by the Doctor, who plans to escort her back to her homeworld. Unfortunately, he discovers that this will mean she will be sentenced to excruciating torture and execution. Can he go through with his plan, if it has this result?

As theatre, this episode is a version of the two enemies 'stuck in a lift' drama, exposing the Doctor's discomfort in the company of 'Margaret', as he delivers her up to this form of 'justice'. The first example of the four 'stuck in a lift' dramas in classic *Doctor Who* was the third story, made up of two episodes called *The Edge of Destruction* and *The Brink of Disaster*, in which the TARDIS itself is the 'lift', and the four stuck in it suffer the dangers of psychological breakdown, as the TARDIS hurtles back in time towards its own doom. The effect of these psychic instabilities (caused by the TARDIS telepathically conveying its sense of acute danger) exacerbates the tensions between the four, which were already high, as Ian and Barbara feel themselves to be kidnap victims of the Doctor, and Susan feels herself torn between sympathy for their plight and loyalty to her grandfather.

In *Boom Town*, the Doctor and his companions cannot look the Slitheen in the eye, because they must feel disquiet at the consequences of their intended actions. The truth is, 'Margaret' is right. They all – even the Doctor – must know that it would be wrong to return her to that fate.

Is the Doctor's justice multicultural or universal?

Should terrorists be deported to countries with that sort of 'justice'? *Boom Town* develops the moral issues arising from *The End of the World*, in the form of local versus universal justice. If the Doctor rejects the arrogance of assuming his culture is best, and tries to affirm all cultures, that leads him to send Blon Slitheen to a dreadful fate. But if he recoils from this, and remembers that there are absolute evils in the universe to be fought (like torture and execution), then what should he do? There appears to be no intergalactic equivalent of the Court at The Hague, even if there might be an equivalent to the Geneva Convention ('The Shadow Proclamation' sounds like this). He could operate summary justice or local justice. As his own people are gone, he can't even appeal to Time Lord justice (should he want to!). In general, the Doctor prevaricates between affirming local justice, operating where he can on the basis of local norms, and absolute, universal justice, where he acts to save planets from megalomaniacs. So, should he send 'Margaret' back to her own planet where her own race's morality rules – where she will suffer a punishment he must think is barbaric and evil?

These difficulties highlight the problems inherent in the Doctor's solution to the tensions between local and universal justice, which we saw revealed by his vigorous riposte to Rose, 'It's a different morality. Get used to it or go home!' The Doctor seems to solve the questions of intergalactic morality by validating local customs. But how far can a universal culture mean a simple tolerance of all ethics (and therefore a pursuit of none)? Or to what extent does it entail trying to discover the ethics relevant for all, for the universe?

These are hardly peripheral issues today, when some US States and all EU States ban torture and execution, but other US States authorise the death penalty. Meanwhile, the UK government struggles with whether it can justify sending those 'glorifying terror' back to régimes which use torture and execution, on the basis of 'agreements' not to do so to those deported from Britain.

> Discussion: When your country implements laws you think are ethically wrong, how far should you tolerate or go along with them in a 'law-abiding' way, and how far should you resist, fight and try to undermine them?

Self-sacrifice

The Doctor is convinced he has a better claim to moral virtue than Rose or any human on the basis not only of an extraordinarily long record of fighting evils, but an even longer record of experiencing and adapting to different worlds and their amazingly varied cultures. In one way, *Father's Day* demonstrates that: Rose thought she was right to save her dad, only to find that the Doctor was right, as her action unleashed the cosmic havoc of the Reapers, causing the deaths of many.

But there is another dimension to this story, of course: the decision by Pete Tyler to act completely out of character, and be the hero who really fixes it for absolutely everyone – at the cost of his own life. His heroic self-sacrifice saves the lives of everyone who had been erased by the Reapers. So it was not the Doctor, but a human being (and a particularly flawed one at that) who saved everyone. And this raises a new moral dimension.

The idea of self-sacrifice is of course far from uncommon in literature – and in *Doctor Who*. Jo Grant's decision to sacrifice herself to save the Doctor in *The Daemons* is good drama. Though, as the authors of *Doctor Who – the Discontinuity Guide* rightly commented, as a plot resolution, it is 'risible'.[4] The idea that an 'amoral' monster like Azal when confronted by Jo's virtue would just have to explode is incredible. But there are many other examples, far truer to experience. In *The End of the World*, Jabe sacrifices herself to enable the Doctor to succeed in raising the defence shield that saves most on board the viewing station. In some stories, some villains or flawed characters atone for their mistakes as they save others' lives at the cost of their own. These include Vaughan, the villain in *The Invasion*; even more clearly, the weak Fewsham in *The Seeds of Death*; and perhaps most controversially Galloway in *Death to the Daleks*, who is effectively a suicide bomber, stowing on board the Dalek ship and blowing himself (and the Daleks) up, and in the process saving the planet Exxilon, and the human race from Dalek destruction. War often involves soldiers in acts of great heroism, as they face terrible risks in saving their comrades. But its context is morally ambiguous, as the next moment they will be acting to destroy others.

The self-sacrifice of Pete includes no such ambiguity. He

---

[4] Paul Cornell, Martin Day and Keith Topping (eds): *Doctor Who: The Discontinuity Guide* (Virgin, 1995) p. 129.

dies that others may live. And that language reminds us, of course, that a clear self-sacrifice lies at the heart of the Christian faith: Jesus dying that we might live. For Christians, there is a further element: Jesus as the Messiah and Son of God dies as the ultimate sacrifice, as the ultimate answer to evil, through whom all our sin is forgiven, all evil quashed.

> Reflection: We often admire the heroism of those who risk losing life to save others. But we do not have to risk our lives to save others. The choices we make in relation to charity can save many lives, without us even having to die to achieve it.

The TARDIS as moral agent

Most surprisingly, perhaps, at the conclusion of *Boom Town*, the TARDIS plays a moral rôle. There are implications for the way in which the TARDIS is increasingly portrayed as a living entity, which we will pursue in a later chapter. But there is one final thought arising out of the way the TARDIS itself solves the Doctor's moral dilemma in *Boom Town*. The Doctor is spared either releasing 'Margaret' or returning her to barbaric conditions: the TARDIS uses time-vector energy to pull her back through her own personal time to being an egg again, ready to live a new life. The moral problem is sidestepped. If only it were so easy in real life! She is hatched again!

Hatched again

One final thought. In one of his most celebrated encounters, Jesus was quizzed by a high-ranking religious figure,

Nicodemus, in relation to which, Jesus said the man needed to be 'born again'. The shock waves of that challenge continue to this day. Nicodemus blusters with a question about the impossibility of re-entering your mother's womb (see John 3:3–5). But here, 'Margaret' does almost exactly that, though her reptilian life-form reverts not into life in the womb, of course, but to its egg stage.

This is science fiction, and so 'Margaret' can make a brand-new start for real. As a demand for us to pursue this form of being born again literally, we cannot comply. But as an image for how radical the change is when we let God truly be God of our lives, it is highly appropriate.

But in some ways the challenge of Jesus is even more radical than the opportunity given to Blon Slitheen. 'Flesh gives birth to flesh, but the Spirit gives birth to spirit' (John 3:6). Even though 'Margaret' is literally hatched again, her new life is still flesh. But Jesus does not call us to repeat this life, even in a better way. His challenge to be 'born again' is to live spiritually. 'Born from above' is another meaning of the famous phrase. Starting not the same life all over again, perhaps making a better go of it, but starting a new form of life. It's as radical as starting again, and even more so, because the new life is life with God at its heart.

11

Sex in the TARDIS

Perhaps the best story of the first new season of *Doctor Who* was two-part story *The Empty Child* and *The Doctor Dances*. The first episode, especially, was full of suspense and growing horror – which we will explore in the next chapter. But this is the story in which sex is a central theme. First, single-parenthood lies at the heart of the story. And second, we have the introduction of companion Captain Jack Harkness, who can be as gung-ho as the Brigadier of old, but with a sexual self-confidence that raises new tensions and issues. From his first dialogue onwards, we have a flow of mild, bisexual repartee.

No hanky-panky in the TARDIS?

The new series as a whole is quite different to the original series in terms of the frequent, if mild sexual innuendo, heterosexual, homosexual and bisexual, from the first episode onwards. But this two-part story not only excels in that regard, but places sexual behaviour (teenage pregnancy) right at the heart of the story.

What is most different about the series in the hands of

Russell T. Davies – apart from being written 40 years on and in a context where mild sexual references are a commonplace in much 'family' drama – is that Davies is a master of what we have called high octane emotional drama. The original series rarely moved to tears; the new series aims and succeeds at that in most episodes. But this involves relationship issues, and it is that which fuels the romantic and sexual dialogue. Rose is the first companion whose relationship with a boyfriend is explored over more than one story. And as Mickey tries to rekindle this relationship (in *Boom Town*, after Rose returns in the TARDIS, six months later), he suggests they spend the night in a hotel together.

The sexual references might pass some viewers by, and I will not mention them all. But an example comes already in the first episode, where we see the Doctor prove his alien reading skills (absorbing a story in a split-second flick through a magazine and dismissing it with a quip: 'That won't last: he's gay and she's an alien!').

The quips in *The Empty Child* and *The Doctor Dances* are frequent and often centre on Captain Jack's bisexual indifference when it comes to dance partners and more. First, he spots Rose dangling from a rope, and comments on her bottom; his RAF colleague thinks he is talking about *him*, and Jack retorts, 'I got to go and meet a girl – but *you* got an excellent bottom too!' Later, when Rose thinks she will be a good 'distraction' for Harkness' RAF colleague, Jack comments that the man has different tastes: Jack would be a better distraction! There are several other passing references to dancing partners of the same or opposite sex which have a mild sexual ambiguity about them. And most strikingly, when Nancy (the single mother at the heart of the story) is cornered by Mr Lloyd, the man she has stolen food from, and he threatens her with the police, she stands up to him, demanding more food – and wire-cutters. It seems absurd for a moment – until, with implied blackmail, she notes the overflow of food during wartime rationing, and mentions that people assume the butcher is 'messing about' with his wife, but she knows that it's Mr Lloyd who's actually having the affair with him.

In addition to all the references that present Captain Jack as bisexual – and a very deliberate and obvious, immediate sexual chemistry between him and Rose – there is the major theme that Nancy, who feels tremendously ashamed, having become a single, underage mum in the 1930s, must affirm Jamie as her son. This moment of truth becomes a healing moment in the most literal sense, as it is the one thing that enables the nanogenes (which have been re-sequencing people's DNA in a catastrophically wrong way) to correct their deadly error and save lives rather than destroy.

These are strong and complex issues, well presented in the story, raising major issues both at a personal and at a social level. They include single-parenthood; honesty about sex; homosexuality and bisexuality; and the far more open nature of family discourse about sexual issues today. *Doctor Who* may still be primarily aimed at its classic audience of 9–14-year-olds, but it is far more mature and adult in the emotional side of the drama, with the result that the nature of relationships is explored far more closely than in the classic series.

That does not mean that sexual issues never arose in the earlier series. Companions sometimes fell in love, kissed and went off into the sunset as it were, including the Doctor's granddaughter Susan, as well as Vicki, Jo and Peri. There was also sexual jeopardy. This was sometimes played for comic effect, as when the Doctor inadvertently proposes to an Aztec lady. But there was also sexual violence, for example where Saxon woman Edith is the victim of Viking attack (a very discreetly implied rape) in *The Time Meddler*, and in *The Crusades*, where Barbara is under threat of rape and torture from El Akir, who captures her for his harem. Also, there is playful banter, for example between Dioni and her Thal boyfriend in *The Daleks*, and between Tanya Lernov and Enrico Casali in *The Wheel in Space*. However, it was much more discreet, and the general content was much less obviously sexual in those stories from the 1960s.

As for the old comment that writers should ensure 'there is no hanky-panky in the TARDIS', has the new series changed the basic rule of no romantic or sexual relationship between the Doctor and companion? Any blurring of this would immediately change the whole quality of everything that happens. That was why the female companion was originally written as a granddaughter, and then as a kind of substitute granddaughter, a ward. So by the time much younger-looking Doctors appeared, the context was clear.

Russell T. Davies himself said it would be death to the series if the Doctor and Rose kissed,[1] and though that did actually happen, the context ensured it worked, as the Doctor gave her a kind of Time Lord's 'kiss of life' but at the expense of his own Ninth incarnation.

---

[1] Russell T. Davies on Billie Piper, in *Radio Times: Doctor Who* (16 page collector's special, 2005), p. 5.

Incidentally, the Eighth Doctor kissed Grace three times in the 1996 film. One wonders whether she would have had to be quickly written out, having dangerously crossed the romantic threshold, if that partnership had successfully re-launched the TV series.

As we have mentioned, the issues opened up in this two-part story include single-motherhood. In Britain, since national registers began in 1837 (and no doubt for a long time before that) until about 1960, about 5 per cent of live births every year took place outside marriage, with the exception of the two World Wars, when the figures grew towards the 10 per cent mark, dropping back again afterwards. Since the 1960s, there has been a strong rise in births outside marriage (now over 40 per cent), not to mention in abortions. Today, cohabitation is extremely widespread, both as a precursor and as an alternative to marriage.

Christians – and any others who want to affirm the value of marriage – are caught in a difficult tension here, with the desire to affirm both the value of marriage, and the value of the child, or indeed the parent, whatever their marital or legitimate status. Jesus himself was notoriously radical on this issue, affirming in the strongest manner a five-times divorced foreign cohabitee (John 4), not to mention a convicted adulteress (John 8) and a presumed prostitute (Luke 7). Yet he successfully did this while also strongly affirming and indeed reinforcing the value of the commitment of marriage. So the principle is not in doubt: somehow we should aim at both affirming the person, whatever their sexual status, and the value of the commitment of marriage.

This means that in the context of the story, we can applaud

the way the Doctor helps Nancy to dare to be honest with and about Jamie. Both Jamie and Nancy need and deserve to be affirmed. But at the same time we can applaud the commitment that would have stood by and with the partner 'till death us do part' rather than abandoning her at the age of '15 or 16'. The love expressed in commitment in marriage also affirms people, and should be proactively supported.

As for the many gay references in the new series, this should not just be put down to Russell T. Davies' personal stance, despite his earlier drama *Queer as Folk* with its over-lapping themes of homosexual lifestyles and *Doctor Who* fans. If this series is compared with today's soaps, or indeed other science fiction dramas broadcast at similar times, it is far from unusual. In practice, the references are still discreet enough for the younger audience to miss them. Meanwhile, *Doctor Who* – and other equivalent dramas – can either be taken as dangerous challenges to be solved by the liberal use of the OFF button, or as opportunities to discuss openly the controversial issues that you can be sure teenagers will be discussing elsewhere. Generally, the opportunity is a very positive one, as teenagers are usually in the process of making up their minds on such issues, rather than offering unchallenge-able certainties. So if parents also discuss the issues raised with a readiness to face awkward or complex questions, rather than presenting fixed answers without recognising the issues, then very helpful discussions can take place.

Incidentally, by the look of it, the same discreetness will probably not be true of the *Doctor Who* spin-off, *Torchwood*, with Captain Jack Harkness, set for BBC3 in 2006, trailed as 'adult' sci-fi, and after the watershed.

As for a more detailed exploration, outlining just what might be said on homosexuality, that would take us well beyond our brief. So we must generalise, very briefly. People generally, typically follow one of four or five approaches, and readers may find themselves identifying clearly with one or other of these.

There are two polar opposite views, which we might describe as homophobic and gay rights. The first rejects not only gay sex but also gay people; the second affirms both unequivocally.

Between those are two or three less polarised views. There are those who reject gay sex but affirm gay people. This is the approach adopted by most evangelicals and catholics.[2] Then there are those who affirm marriage as the ideal and the norm, but admit that for some people in our broken, fallen world, heterosexual marriage is not possible, and they should be permitted gay relationships in a context approximating to the commitment of marriage. This approach is probably taken by most liberal Christians, and a much smaller number of evangelicals and catholics.[3] And finally of course, there will be those whose response is somewhere between these last two.

---

[2] For evangelicals, see the ACUTE (Evangelical Alliance Commission on Unity and Truth among Evangelicals) report, *Faith Hope and Homosexuality* (Paternoster, 1998). Roman Catholic encyclicals have up to now taken a similar approach, but news items suggest the Vatican under new Pope, Benedikt XVI, is seriously considering whether to urge Roman Catholics to bar from the priesthood not only those in homosexual relationships, but also those of homosexual orientation who are strictly celibate. See BBC News website reports for 23 September 2005.

[3] Rowan Williams, the Archbishop of Canterbury, for example, has written views approximating to this.

There will be those who switch between these two views – I have met many Christians who have found it difficult to reach the conclusion that clinches all doubts on this issue, as each answer leaves a different question unresolved. And there are mediating or ambiguous approaches. For example, the pastor who firmly believes that sex outside marriage is always wrong, including gay sex, but who would counsel the obviously gay man strongly against a particular possibility of heterosexual marriage, recognising the possible disaster for the couple, and turning a blind eye to the consequence that the gay man might end up in a gay relationship instead.

Discussion: If Captain Jack Harkness (or someone like him) came to you, or to your counsellor or pastor for advice on whether to attempt to change his bisexual flirtatiousness, what would you say or want them to say to him?

12

Horror, Fangs and Suspense

Horror

In the *Doctor Who* TV stories, *Horror of Fang Rock* alone has 'horror' in its title, but is far from the only horror story in classic *Doctor Who,* and the series is replete with fangs of ravenous Drashigs, Androgums, not to mention vampires, and of course dangers and threats of hundreds of different types. And the new series has continued this, especially in the episode *The Empty Child,* the first of a two-part story, which not only provides an element of horror, but also suspense. The threat faced turns out to be an accident, caused by malfunctioning technology, and we will return to that dimension in the next chapter.

Suspense

The Empty Child was without a doubt one of the strongest episodes of the new series. This was because of the strong development of suspense – which is not the same as horror.

Doctor Who is not without its horror elements, too. However, as the series is aiming at U, PG or at most 12 ratings, pure horror scenes worthy of a 15 or 18 are pulled or softened. In fact, horror as such is incidental to *Doctor Who* at its best. The best 'horror' is not blood and gore, but implied. For me, as a child, one of the most chilling scenes of the classic series was a sequence in *The Dalek Invasion of Earth* – and it was not one of those where Daleks exterminate on screen. There is a moment when Susan and her friend David are shockingly interrupted by a Dalek off-screen ordering some unseen man to stop, and the sounds of his desperate plea followed by the sound of exterminating Dalek fire and the final scream. In many ways, that was more unsettling than the on-screen attacks, because it engaged the imagination more fully, especially as the screen centred on Susan's traumatised reaction.

The Empty Child has its horrific moments, but in one of them – the moment when Dr Constantine mutates into the welded gas-mask sub-human being – the original idea of adding the sound of cracking bones was immediately seen as too horrific, and pulled.[1] But that scene is not what gives this episode its 'behind the sofa' quality. It's the build-up of suspense, and the sense of a world going wrong.

The cliff-hanger

The Empty Child was one of only three episodes with a cliff-hanger in season one of the new series. The first was *Aliens of London*. But having set up the first cliff-hanger, it immediately

---

[1] As *Doctor Who Magazine #358* noted, this was a decision during production, not as suggested in the tabloids, after transmission for the DVD (20 July 2005), p. 7.

undid the suspense by showing the Doctor alive in 'next week on *Doctor Who*'! The 'next week' feature is of course intended to whet the appetite and draw people back next week, like the cliff-hanger did. So when there *is* a cliff-hanger, the programme makers must avoid answering the question so nicely set up. *The Empty Child* and *Bad Wolf* reduced this mistake, but not enough, and the viewer who wanted to have the rare experience of the suspense of a genuine cliff-hanger had to block their ears and eyes, or rush to switch off immediately.

The cliff-hanger, of course, was a key feature in the classic series, and is the most significant loss in the new series. The function of this was to raise the temperature, of course, deepening concern for our heroes. It also heightened the sense of mystery and puzzlement, for often the cliff-hanger was not simply the Doctor and/or companions in jeopardy, but a sense of perplexity: what *is* going on? Mostly, the resolutions simply unlocked the puzzle quite easily, adding little to the plot. But at their best, they drove the action forward powerfully. For me, the all-time best cliff-hanger came at the end of episode one of *The Caves of Androzani*, where the guns blaze in order to execute the Doctor and his companion, Peri. Our sense of desperate concern and puzzlement is actually heightened by the resolution, where we see the guns blazing – and then see the Doctor and Peri slump, dead! (And if you haven't seen this story, I won't spoil it by explaining the rest of it!)

Also, the new series has not achieved that high standard of plot resolution (though, to be fair, the classic series often provided weak solutions of the 'and with one bound, he was free' variety). Both *Boom Town* and the resolution of the cliff-hanger at the start of *The Parting of the Ways*, as well as the final resolution of that story allow a simple use of technology to solve the scriptwriters' troubles, an almost literal *Deus ex machina*[2] which is fatal not only for the immediate context, but also for the longer-term prospects of the series. If the TARDIS can now dematerialise around the threatened companion at will, then all threats against them seem empty. If the TARDIS has such awesome epoch-rewriting power that it can reverse people's lives (*Boom Town*) and raise the dead (presumably including the entire implicitly exterminated population of Earth at the end of *The Parting of the Ways*), then the Doctor could after all take the machine to the critical moment in the 'Time War', unleash the heart and soul of the TARDIS on himself, and at the mere cost of his tenth regeneration, reverse the polarities of time, and bring back all the destroyed Time Lords, while using this awesome time-vector energy to turn all Daleks and other foes to dust. And if the Master had had access to such power. . .

The classic series by and large eschewed simple technical fixes to plot-lines and cliff-hangers, and the new series must learn to follow suit.

Christians and horror

Some might think that the only Christian interest in horror and suspense – indeed, the only moral or social interest generally

---

[2] Literally this means 'God out of the box' and is a time-honoured description of the worst kind of plot-resolution, where something powerful is artificially produced out of thin air to resolve the plot. It has no validity in the story's build up, and cheats the reader or viewer by suddenly introducing a magic solution to the drama.

– concerns the issues of screen violence and censorship. Far from it. Story lies at the heart of the Bible. Now, although there are many fictional stories (the parables, for example), the Bible majors in story rooted in fact. But this is narrative with a purpose – significant history. The story can operate at the grand level (what postmodern interpreters call 'metanarratives'),[3] the story of creation, and redemption. It can also be a particular story – about a king, prophet or disciple, for example. And in these biblical narratives we certainly see a range of factors like horror, suspense, irony, absurdity, and so on, not to mention prophecy and fulfilment, which is one of the most dramatic factors of many good science fiction stories.

There are many stories in the Bible which, if filmed as described, would merit the 18 that Mel Gibson's *The Passion* was given. Commentators on *Doctor Who* sometimes discuss the 'body count' – the number of people killed in the course of a story. This horror dimension is however matched in the Bible, particular the histories and prophecies of the Old Testament, where there are many stories and prophecies of 'many, many bodies – flung everywhere' (Amos 8:3). Armageddon is after all a biblical word (Revelation 16:16).

Why is horror in the Bible? It has a purpose, and it is not for entertainment. The biblical stories trade in integrity – integrity to the facts, to the motives, to the significance. And biblical writers will not let embarrassment about the facts oblige them to censor the truth. Heroes like David, Moses, Elijah, Peter

---

[3] Jean-François Lyotard: *The Postmodern Condition* (1979), Eng. tr: by G Bennington & B. Massumi (Manchester University Press, 1984), p. *xxiv*.

and Paul are shown with their greatest failures exposed. Even Jesus, the Messiah, is not exempt from this utter integrity of narrative. If at Gethsemane, Jesus prayed with desperation to avoid the oncoming suffering, with sweat pouring down from him, this struggle which some might see as weakness is not censored; if at Golgotha, on the cross, he prayed, 'My God, my God, why have you forsaken me?' (Mark 15:34), which many might find disquieting, the Gospels do not cut it from their accounts. And the horror is recorded because it is a terrible part of the reality. The horror is there not to distract from the main point of the story but to highlight it.

Doctor Who and fiction generally does itself a service when horror and other disturbing factors are included not for their own sake, but to highlight the reality of the drama.

Discussion: To what extent does it make sense to encourage children to begin to face the horrors that an evil world can inflict?

Do we protect ourselves – or our children – by keeping quiet about terrible evils?

13

The Living TARDIS

Biotechnology

While *Doctor Who* has mostly kept its technobabble restricted to 'reversing the polarities', the odd bit of chaotic rewiring, and fantastical ideas of sonic screwdrivers, fluid links, and trans-mat beams, it has had technological assumptions guiding it, and these have been slowly changing. The shift, as we shall see, is towards the increasing recognition that technology is not simply a matter of ever more complex machines, but includes the impact of biotechnology. This has increasingly reshaped the way the TARDIS is seen, especially in the new series, but also other storylines, especially in the two-part story *The Empty Child* and *The Doctor Dances*, with which we start.

The curse of fatal life

The science fiction concept – that nanogenes with a benign remit released into the environment could go wrong and cause a biological disaster – is far from unimaginable. Prince

Charles caused some controversy back in 2003 by speaking his mind on nanotechnology, recognising potential benefits but cautioning us to beware the dangers that could follow. He was widely quoted as decrying the possibility of nanorobots going off the rails and reducing all organic matter (including all humans, of course) to 'grey goo'. (He denied saying this.) As with many of the Prince of Wales' expressions of opinion, many are quick to criticise, perhaps even believing that he should not be allowed to express opinions on anything interesting or relevant at all. Others tackle the issues, defending their corners – in this case, those who are at early stages of this potential revolution and, like Lord May, president of the Royal Society, reply that the 'grey goo' disaster is even less likely to happen than building a real Jurassic Park. A third group, with those like Sir Martin Rees, Astronomer Royal, suggest that such concerns are not relevant for another 50 years yet, in other words the danger is only science fiction for now, but not impossible in the very long term.

In science fiction itself, the danger is of course greatly accelerated if, as here, future technologies are introduced by advanced aliens. But the implied social and cultural issues are much the same: could science and technology take a disastrous wrong turn, leading the human race down an inescapable cul-de-sac to disaster? The idea of the danger of irreversible damage to the environment is the major case against genetically modified foods, of course. This presses things a stage further: not just microscopic robots, but in due course genetically modified bacteria and the like. Much of this arena is still science fiction – but science fiction at its best can go beyond mere entertainment, and raise real issues for the long term.

Because *Doctor Who* at its best repeatedly places our heroes in jeopardy, the possibilities of science and technology going wrong crop up more frequently than those going well. Many of the monster races are products of warped, mistaken or flawed technologies. Daleks were humanoids, now genetically modified as bio-weapons; Sontarans are cloned to be the ultimate soldiers; and Cybermen were humanoids, now bionically and cybernetically augmented to the point of no return for their humanity. Other dangers are posed by arrogant scientists, or of course sentient computers. However, the Doctor himself uses science and technology to rescue the situations caused by their degeneration or abuse.

We return, theologically, to the importance of the Fall: science or technology can never be our saviour, for all our experience shows all technologies can be used both for good and for evil. We live in a world with creative possibilities, but in a fallen world where selfish drives abuse such powers. The new series of *Doctor Who* strengthens an understated feature of the classic series: the Doctor is not simply a Superman, a mythic saviour-figure; he is also an inspiration. As we have seen, the encounter with the Doctor changes Rose. And in the final episode of this first new season, it is changing Mickey and Jackie, too, lifting them beyond their personal desire to save (and keep) Rose, and on to working together to save the (future) world.

This is an excellent mythic picture: we need a saviour not simply to rescue us from the consequences of our mistakes, as if we should ignore our responsibility in the world, but also to inspire us to play our rôle within it. Or, to use more technical theological terms, for Christians, our salvation through Jesus

Christ as Saviour includes two major dimensions: 'justification' (being put right with God, saved from sin, etc.) and 'sanctification' (being inspired to become more right before God, growing away from selfishness and more ready to care for others, and so on). For Christians, Christ not only forgives, but also inspires. So scientists or indeed nanotechnologists who are Christian do not simply look to Christ to forgive them their faults, whether conventional or catastrophic; they are inspired to follow and imitate Christ, seeking to pursue their technological innovations in ways that look most likely to enhance life.

Relative dimensions

What is the TARDIS? Some answers to this remain constant throughout *Doctor Who*. It stands for 'Time And Relative Dimensions In Space'. The TARDIS is a somewhat dated (by Gallifreyan standards) machine for transporting its passengers through time and space. When it is working properly, it has directional steering, so the Doctor can make it land broadly where and when he wants to. It also has a 'chameleon circuit,' through which the TARDIS disguises itself shortly before landing into a form which blends unobtrusively with its environment. Unfortunately, the Doctor's TARDIS has been faulty in that respect since landing in 1963, always materialising as a Police Box (except for a brief exchange of forms in *Attack of the Cybermen*).

But what the TARDIS actually is, and how we should think about it, has been subtly changing over the years. The original descriptions of it, together with its appearance with gleaming white panels, present the 1960s 'technological revolution' advanced to the ultimate degree. It is, originally, a machine of the most technically advanced type imaginable.

However, as we have seen, already by *The Edge of Destruction* (1964), the TARDIS was incipiently shown to have a telepathic dimension. The story shows bizarre events, which trigger paranoia. However, in the end, Barbara's intuition proves right: the TARDIS was actively communicating danger in a rudimentary and also partly telepathic way. This ability was apparently news even to the Doctor, who had only treated it as a clever machine. Perhaps we should not be surprised, as the Time Lord race are also shown to have this telepathic dimension as the series progresses (and were always intended to, with Susan supposedly having such skills in enhanced measure in the original conception).

In *The Masque of Mandragora* (1976) we saw an alternative control room, with its own console, a room far less gleaming and white, and some other Fourth and Fifth Doctor stories began to explore other rooms inside the TARDIS. A darker or larger control room 'could' be another part of this extraordinary ship.

However, it was the film of 1996 with the Eighth Doctor that fundamentally changed the TARDIS' appearance into something not too far from its current form: grand, darker and far more organic. What's more, where it comes to awesome power with a telepathic dimension, there is more than a hint of similarity between the 'Eye of Harmony' in that TARDIS, and the 'heart of the TARDIS' in the current series, even if they are placed in different parts of the craft.

This organic dimension has been greatly accentuated in the

current series, not only in appearance but also in reality, as we shall see. I think there is a symbolic significance in this. In 1963, and for a while afterwards, the TARDIS was conceived as a spectacular achievement of futuristic technological engineering. The problems of nuclear physics were, for Time Lords, opportunities. So the TARDIS technology involved in time flight was supposed to be unlocked by harnessing the powers of supernovae. We can add to this picture that science fiction concerns of early stories homed in on issues of radiation and nuclear technology, static electricity, computers taking over and the like. But over the years, the biological dimension has become stronger. As we saw earlier, the Daleks were originally just victims of physical processes of radioactive effects of mutation, but were later reconceived as also genetically modified. The TARDIS was early on seen as telepathic, and indeed telepathic races featured early with *The Sensorites* (1964). But the biological dimension in *Doctor Who* was modest to start off with, with giant insects on Vortis (*The Web Planet* – 1965), and the deadly effects of the common cold in a future culture long free from exposure to it (*The Ark* – 1966). But after that, biotechnological issues cropped up increasingly, with the Cybermen (1966), Nestene bioplastic (1970), Silurian use of biological warfare (1970), Sontaran clones (1972) and GM Daleks (1975), for example. So, the change in conception of the Daleks – from the physics-based idea of radioactively mutated organisms to the biologically driven concept of a deliberate act of genetic engineering on top of that mutation – also illustrates the shift of focus from physics and conventional mechanical technology to biology and organic technology.

The concept of the TARDIS as a living thing has also been developing as an implicit theme for some time. The Second Doctor communicates telepathically with the Time Lords, as he summons them to solve massive breaches of time travelling in *The War Games* (and fails to escape their bureaucratic clutches). After this, for such communication, the Third Doctor uses the 'telepathic circuits' of the TARDIS. The Third Doctor also talks of the TARDIS in personal terms. For example, in *The Time Monster* he talks of the 'mood' of the TARDIS, and Jo quizzes him about treating the TARDIS 'as if she was alive'. The Doctor says that it depends what she means, but then makes a parallel with his car, 'Bessie'.

In the 1996 film, the Master says that the TARDIS 'likes' Chang Lee, as the TARDIS opens up its 'Eye of Harmony' to his gaze. However, whether this is meant symbolically, or in a strong, telepathic sense is not made clear. More clearly, the Doctor himself comments that the TARDIS is 'a sentimental old thing' after it acts to reverse the deaths of Grace and Chang, and closes its Eye of Harmony as he and Grace embrace. This saving of Grace and Chang is the closest the classic series got to showing the powers Rose will use when taken over by its 'vortex energy' in *The Parting of the Ways*, as she brings Jack back from death.

Now this living dimension is much more explicitly deliberate and fully biological in this new series. The TARDIS is a player that can activate the judgement on 'Margaret Blaine' and actually achieve the result that not just 'Margaret' but also the Doctor was looking for.

The living ship is of course not unknown in popular science fiction. It was a major theme with 'Moya' in *Farscape*.

Similarly, in *Babylon 5*, Vorlon ships were also living vessels. This development in *Doctor Who* reflects the way in which the cutting edge of science and also our technological nightmares have shifted focus from physics, by and large, to biology: 50 years ago, the relatively new threat of nuclear annihilation, contrasted with the extraordinary positive technical achievements in sending men to the Moon, saw the cutting edge closer to physics; today, the sequencing of the human genome, breakthroughs in cloning, biotechnology and bioweapons have shifted both the optimistic and pessimistic focus for science, and therefore also for science fiction, towards biology.

As a result of such changes, we are all going to have to get used to the issues of genetic engineering and the like increasingly requiring urgent work. New areas of ethical conflict need to be worked through.

Cloning and genetics – the spiritual challenge

To some extent, this shift from physics to biology is a response to the most far-reaching scientific discovery in the second half of the twentieth century, namely that of the structure of DNA in 1952. As a result, we are now very aware of genetic diseases and conditions, and moral debates about stem-cell research, or about babies born to be genetically compatible donors for siblings, are not science fiction but regular fare. If I can declare a personal interest, as having a son with Down's Syndrome, we can also see how this breakthrough in genetics changed perceptions of that condition. John Langdon Down, the Victorian pioneer who first recognised the cluster of diagnostic elements as exemplifying this condition, assumed the cause was an evolutionary throw-back to what he considered a primitive 'Mongolian' phase in evolution, from which the earlier label 'Mongol' derived. As late as 1924, scientists were reworking this evolutionary analysis, arguing the condition was a throw-back to the orang-utang, and the diagnostic 'simian crease' (on hand or foot) reflects this phase in analysis.[1]

But in 1959, the cause of Down's syndrome was discovered to be genetic – a trisomy of chromosone 21 (or, rarely, a partial mosaic or partial translocation). The advances in science and medicine have thrown this to the forefront of the abortion debate, with our Western societies mostly sanctioning abortion of such babies, arguably an early step in the drift towards 'designer babies'. Both 'therapeutic cloning' and 'reproductive cloning' heighten these issues.

Start talking about cloning, genetic engineering, designer babies and the like, and most people, whether Christian or not, begin to think of the possible dangers ahead. As science fiction dreams up worlds where people have been overthrown by the soldiers they clone (and elements of this can be found in *Doctor Who*, *Star Trek* and *Star Wars*, for example), we assume the only sensible response is to want to slam on the brakes.

However, a Christian perspective should start with the positive side first. Jesus himself proclaimed that his messianic mission would be centred on healing (Luke 4). What's more,

---

[1] G. F. Smith and J. M. Berg: *Downs Anomaly* (1966; 2nd ed: Longman, Churchill Livingstone Medical Division, 1976), pp.1–4.

in the Greek of the New Testament, the same word *sōtēria* is sometimes translated salvation, sometimes healing, since in the Bible the work of salvation is not limited to the spiritual aspect, or to the afterlife, but is also God's active work in healing now. Jesus told John the Baptist to look at these acts of healing as the sign that he was fulfilling his messianic call (Matthew 11:1–6). This emphasis on healing continued in the Acts and throughout Christian history, with the development of care for the sick, founding of hospitals and the like. So Christians will want to welcome and work with factors that bring healing, so long as they are not compromised by ethical shortcomings.

Nonetheless, we cannot ignore these ethical problems. A consumerist society is inclined to take the possibilities of genetic intervention in a consumerist direction, and it is right to challenge the search for the 'perfect baby' as a consumerist pathology. Too often, people see in their children the expression of their own selfish desires or fears, and this is deeply corrupting.

As for cloning, the danger is not initially that we might clone an army of 'perfect soldiers' like the Sontarans (*The Time Warrior*) or Drahvins (*Galaxy 4*), but might want to clone for altogether more laudable reasons. These include: helping those desperate for babies (such as infertile couples or some gay couples); facilitating transplantation tissue; replicating a lost and dearly loved child; cloning unique geniuses (who would then not be so unique!). Also, there are people in religious cults, such as the Raelians, who promote cloning.

Most of our responses are either emotive or rationalist. Many respond to such issues with a heartfelt 'yuk!' But a simple emotional response will not help us work through the pros and cons. The opposite response is to elevate reason. But reason can't solve this problem, because it involves the question of appropriate values, and reason can't generate values; it either works without them, or assumes them. As we saw in Chapter 10, attempts to determine what is truly right or wrong simply by reason didn't work. The attempt to base values on provable absolutes failed, and the attempt to solve this problem by a pragmatic approach fared no better.

As for the Christian response to these questions of values and ethical choices, this operates not on the basis of emotion alone, nor reason alone, nor both together, nor from absolutes, nor pragmatic choices, but from God. As Paul put it: 'be transformed by the renewing of your mind. Then you will be able to test and approve what God's will is – his good, pleasing and perfect will' (Romans 12:2).

14

Blasphemers Will Be Exterminated!

Bad Wolf

Bad Wolf and its resolution, *The Parting of the Ways*, brought season one of the new series to a climax, and with it also brought the 'Bad Wolf' story arc to a clear conclusion. The season's themes, the Time War, the death of all Daleks and Time Lords, the mystery of 'Bad Wolf', and the degeneration of Satellite Five, all come together. But even as the themes coalesce, they undermine the season's certainties. It is one thing to have one almost destroyed Dalek somehow slip through the Time War, but for an emperor to survive and build a whole fleet brings into doubt the finality of the Time War. Perhaps another Time Lord or two may have survived, for example. And as we saw, *Bad Wolf* raised issues of corrupting the media to enslave the society again. However, unlike in *The Long Game*, this was only a step to the goal of total extermination of the human race – the clandestine aim of the Emperor Dalek.

'Do not blaspheme!'

But now we have the curiosity of Daleks chanting 'Do not blaspheme!' – the first hint of a religious dimension to these creatures since the day that Davros their creator declared that inventing such invincible war-creatures would put him 'among the gods', because it would enable him to have god-like powers (in an extraordinary scene in *Genesis of the Daleks*, where Davros argues the merits of genocide!).

It is almost a first for *Doctor Who* – certainly in its TV form – to have Daleks, or advanced aliens of any kind, ordering: 'Do not blaspheme!' Up to now, in *Doctor Who*, aliens issuing such an order would invariably be primitive – with one exception that I can recall (Monarch, the leading Urbankan in *Four to Doomsday*, who, like the Emperor Dalek, conceives himself as God, and questioning him as blasphemy). But, as we have seen, the challenges of religion in our age are not made by animists, but by those well immersed in our modern technical world. If one thinks of bin Laden and his network, for example, the use of the Internet has been a vital part of their whole strategy.

Perhaps having the ultimate, advanced, super-intelligent but compulsively evil Daleks chanting: 'Do not blaspheme!' is a first recognition in *Doctor Who* that in our world, religion can play a positive or a destructive rôle – but as a contemporary force, rather than a primitive one.

Many people are still wedded to an essentially nineteenth-century understanding of the nature of religion, inspired by social thinkers Auguste Comte (around the 1830s) and Karl Marx (from the 1840s), seeing it as a passing phase soon to be outdated as scientific or economic truth takes hold. Whether formally linked to an evolutionary theory or not, a dogma of social evolution is most commonly assumed by those who continue to think of religion in this way. In other words, they assume that mankind used to be primitive in its religion, then developed sophisticated monotheistic religions, but that it will mature and replace such myths with the truths of science.[1] *Doctor Who* has had many writers, and has been less obviously moulded into this view of religious history than *Star Trek*, of course; and so, for example, we see traces of Buddhism in several stories like *Kinda, Snakedance* and *Planet of the Spiders*, and Christianity in *The Romans*.[2] But this outlook does lie behind the usual picture of religion in classic *Doctor Who*, showing it as a broadly animistic, 'primitive' and regressive cultural aberration, or else as a genuine feature of ancient societies.

---

[1] To be a bit more precise, Comte and Marx also saw a middle stage between the age of religion and their visionary futures, both connecting this intermediate phase to some extent with the French Revolution. For Marx that was a 'bourgeois' stage, for Comte, a 'metaphysical phase'. Marx's oft-quoted dictum of religion as 'the opium of the people' was written in his 'Contribution to the Critique of Hegel's *Philosophy of Right*' in 1844, and his theory of economic history and future was set out with Friedrich Engels in *The Communist Manifesto* (1848). Comte's ideas were presented in his *Cours de Philosophie Positive* (1830–42).

[2] Readers keen to explore the comparison between *Star Trek's* more ideologically driven take on religion (especially in the era Gene Roddenberry was in charge), and the more incidentally variegated approach of *Doctor Who* (not to mention the very interestingly different and more credible interpretation of *Babylon 5*) can consult the relevant chapters of my earlier book, *A Closer Look at Science Fiction* (Kingsway, 2001).

But this is the first story I can think of (from the TV stories) where we meet active religious attitudes in an alien species more advanced than we are today. This speaks of a different attitude to the history of religion. Instead, a growing assumption is that religion will not inevitably·die out everywhere; rather, it will change shape. Some religions may decline, but others will grow. That would mean that we should assume that religions will still be flourishing in the twenty-second century and afterwards.

So the question changes shape. The old evolutionary atheist secularism assumed the future was bound to be atheistic, so its question was: 'How do we speed up the process?' Marx and Comte promoted their different ideas, and Stalin and others tried to enforce such atheism.

If we now recognise that religions will continue and develop, then the question becomes: 'What religious visions should we support?' It can, of course, take the negative form: 'What religious visions should we resist or avoid?'

Religious Daleks are of course no more attractive than their secular predecessors! It is no added comfort to know that one is being exterminated for blaspheming the Emperor Dalek instead of simply for being human. But religion can, in the real world, be a powerful motivating force for good or evil. Religious creatures that want to exterminate all heretics or blasphemers should rightly be pilloried as being like Daleks. Those on the other hand who aim to inspire unbelievers towards faith by expressing their own faith in such a way that people are affirmed and positively transformed create the opposite prospect. And it is no bad thing to be reminded that religion can be a force for profound evil, and we must resist that evil, and choose to seek to live out the faith in the way that brings the best hope, faith and love for humanity.

Discussion: Do you think religious faith can be a force for evil? Can it be a force for good?

How do we ensure any expression of religious faith in our lives is more a force for good than for evil?

15

Return of the Cybermen

The Christmas Invasion and season two

At the time of writing, filming for season two is well underway, beginning with a Christmas special with the invasion of Santa Claus (or rather, the evil Sycorax). But it's the return of the Cybermen midway through the season that is the most trailed feature. As far as my sons Stephen and Alex are concerned, it's not the Daleks but the Cybermen who were the scariest monsters; and, as already mentioned, for Russell T. Davies himself, it was the Cybermen who prompted those nightmares.

So who are the Cybermen, and why are they so scary?

Who are the Cybermen?

In the world of *Doctor Who* (according to the first Cybermen story, *The Tenth Planet*), Earth once had a 'twin' planet, Mondas, which we could perhaps think of as once existing in the same orbit, like Jupiter's Trojans (asteroids in the same orbit as Jupiter). But despite being almost a mirror image of Earth, 'somehow' the Mondasians developed differently, succeeding in taking control of the orbit of their world and moving it 'to the edge of space' – which should probably be thought of as the far edge of our solar system. But then they hit trouble and returned to plunder the Earth. Through these millennia, its inhabitants had made two major technological changes to their previously humanoid race: firstly, they exchanged corruptible body parts with mechanical replacements, made of plastic, metal and the like, exploiting these changes to the nth degree; and secondly, as their brains were similarly augmented, altered or replaced, they ensured that their new brains were cybernetically linked. Probably the best way to imagine this is to conceive them replacing or developing their brains technologically in such a way as to upload the entire intellectual Internet world of the Cybermen (let us dub this the 'Cybernet') into a CyberController who acts as a sole Cybernet Service Provider and Command Centre for the whole race of Cybermen.

So we have an organic race with certain vestigial organic elements still intact, but with technology so overwhelming, particularly in its cybernetic capacities, that the race has become ex-human. In particular, they have lost all emotional ability, and believe this to be a great advantage. What this means is that the Cybermen represent a threat at a whole string of different levels.

What is the cyber-threat?

1. Like many other monsters, they often threaten to invade our planet, killing all who get in their way.

2. Being shorn of all emotion, they are amoral. For

example, no deal done with a Cyberman will be honoured, as they have no sense of honour (another 'useless emotion'). Everything will simply be calculated mathematically, and the most advantageous course adopted. An enemy so utterly mathematically ruthless, with no hint of fear or compassion, no 'human weakness', appears to have a military advantage. That is certainly how the Cybermen see it.

3. They use their cybernetic skills to transmit thought-control electric bolts, stunning people into hypnotic submission. This feature was particularly prominent in the earlier Cybermen stories (personally, I believe this made good drama, as it highlighted their distinctively Cybernetic threat). Typically (since this thought-control was apparently too weak to operate out of their close range), they would use metal brackets pinned to humans to augment such cyber-control over distances.

4. Most creepily, they threaten to turn ordinary human beings into a new race of Cybermen, making us into them. They would surgically alter the human body in a variety of ways, and critically, ultimately want to adapt the human brain to ensure it can interface seamlessly with what we have termed the 'Cybernet'. In the stories where this was attempted – with Toberman in The Tomb of the Cybermen for example – they did not properly succeed, suggesting the sort of difficulties that happen when incompatible technologies (or humanities) are integrated.

Mondas

Mondas was the Cybermen's original planet – 'an old name for Earth', and deliberately a take on the Latin name 'mundus' meaning world. The idea of Mondas (if we ignore the far-fetched notion of driving planets to the edge of space and back again, like cars) is part of an old science fiction device which does something very important. It asks: What if our human race were to develop in a different way? The SF way is to picture a parallel Earth, the same in all respects except one. *Star Trek* was full of these – and even devised characteristic technobabble to explain why there were so many planets almost like Earth ('Hodgkins Law of Parallel Planet Development'!), not to mention a 'mirror' universe.

Only once did *Doctor Who* run with the idea of a whole-sale parallel universe, in which all our heroes turn into villains, and wear beards, eye-patches and leather (*Inferno*)!

Alternative Earth-histories with Hitler winning the war (so beloved of *Star Trek*) are not typical of *Doctor Who* either. *Doctor Who* shapes all this in a completely different way. As can be seen in the episode *Fathers Day*, instead of the time paradoxes of *Star Trek*, *Doctor Who* (at least in its current forms) presents a breakdown of time, with the irruption of chronological monsters and the like.

The way *Doctor Who* presents alternative worlds is by showing the long-term consequences of previously human races and others making gigantic mistakes. We saw this approach with the Daleks of the planet Skaro. And now with Mondas we have an even clearer case of this sub-genre, for Mondas is a clear-cut 'parallel Earth'. And it poses the question: What if the human race made a catastrophic error of judgement in its technological development, and allowed technology so to develop that it controlled us, and we became cyborgs?

Cyber-technology versus humanity

What the idea of the Cybermen presents in a very striking way is one of the most awkward questions for our culture: Is the development of science and technology amoral? In other words, neither moral nor immoral, but exempt from moral concerns?

Now the conventional wisdom in our culture is that science and technology should not be confused by value-judgements. This works on the simplistic basis that science is truth, that values can create bias against some truths, and that technology is merely the practical application of scientific discoveries. That pitches science and technology as amoral, as morally neutral, but also positions them as requiring this neutrality to be vigorously defended. In other words, the one permissible value is promoting the importance of value-free science and technology.

But the idea of Cybermen raises the alarming possibility that if we don't guide our science and technology by moral values we may take such a wrong turn that we end up destroying our essential humanity. The idea that this would be perfectly acceptable, that science and technology would win out, that logical consistency requires us to allow technology to reshape our lives without letting emotions and values restrict its advance is of course the philosophy of the Cybermen. If we recoil at it (and we do!), then we conclude that those fallible human emotions and values do after all have a veto on unacceptable developments in science and technology. The Cybermen present a warning: do not let your love of the power available in science and technology result in the destruction of your humanity; do not let its myth of infallible truth deceive you.

Of course, there are all sorts of applications in the current world. We have faced the nuclear threat for 60 years and, as we have seen, biological and genetic developments raise new possibilities. Medical benefit is very often presented as the reason for technological innovations. Cloning of human beings for research to eliminate diseases is one case in point, for as I write, the decision is being seriously considered in the UK to authorise a degree of genetic engineering whereby an embryo would come from a mother altered with genetic material from another, to eliminate mitochondrial diseases. The Cybermen in *Doctor Who* are a race that chose to eliminate diseases and rejected any moral qualms that got in the way. They are a warning that a critical limit could possibly be crossed.

Of course, the problems of amoral science and technology do not require the moral alternative to be a rejection of scientific and technological progress – to be Luddite, fearful and backward-looking. What it requires is the use of judgements suffused with strong, positive moral values. It means that technological possibility has no automatic right, and that perceptive, critical judgement is essential in avoiding destructive wrong turns in our future development.

For Christians, this whole issue is rooted in our understanding of our place in creation. We are not gods, nor the plaything of gods, but created by God, and granted stewardship of the world (Genesis 1:28–31). As scientific and technological possibilities increase, our responsibilities increase with them. We have opportunities to pollute, or to care for the environment. Maybe this will shape the long-term response to events like the devastation of New Orleans and remind us that issues of climate change and stewardship of the planet are vital. Similarly, technology raises new medical possibilities which present tough dilemmas not only in relation to genetic testing of children and other antenatal issues, but also to the range of issues connected with research, funding and medical intervention for those facing mortal illnesses. Christian technologists will want to weigh potential benefits with other effects, respecting life and humanity, while fostering healing.

Cybernet and Internet

I pictured the cybernetic developments of the Cybermen as an aberration in the development of their 'Cybernet'. The intellectual breadth may be there, the knowledge in the databanks, but the freedom that is an aspect of humanity has been sacrificed for technological and perhaps military advantage. An Internet under one person's sole control, and into which we were all compulsorily plugged, taking our orders from Cybercontrol, is a ghastly nightmare. The Internet we have is at the opposite pole to that, providing an engine for freedom. But what kind of freedom does the Internet enable?

Although the Internet is so different from the Cybernet that we see pictured in the Cyber-race, this does not mean that we can simply assume that the freedom driven through the Internet is healthy. In practice, the freedom expressed in the World Wide Web does not come from a healthy inner freedom but often from compulsive drives. This has been explored often enough as the worry that the Internet provides the freedom for pornography of all types to be promoted. More recently, we have been made aware that the Internet has enabled the 'freedom' to train suicide bombers.

To be free of Cybercontrol is only partial freedom. We too often believe that if we are free from outside control we will be truly free. But true freedom cannot come unless we are inwardly free. If we are driven by addictive patterns of behaviour or by violent rage, then being free from outside control will not make us free but merely enable our inner unfreedom to vent itself.

The apostle Paul acknowledged the pull of inner drives which mean that our superficial freedom hides an inner slavery to sin (Romans 7). The apostle Peter challenged: 'Live as free men, but do not use your freedom as a cover-up for evil' (1 Peter 2:16). Jesus himself challenged us to seek this truer, deeper freedom: 'If the Son sets you free, you will be free indeed' (John 8:36).

Cybercontrol

One recurring feature of the earlier Cybermen stories which gave them added impact, I feel, was the theme of Cybercontrol. The Cybermen had somehow learned the art of telepathic control (over short distances). This raises the whole issue in a characteristic SF manner of thought-control – or, as we often term it, 'brainwashing'.

How does such brainwashing occur, and what are the antidotes to it? In *Doctor Who* and SF generally, it is usually achieved either by technological means (as by the Cybermen) or by paranormal powers (as by the Master, a renegade Time Lord who is – or was – certainly a master of hypnosis).

Hypnosis is certainly an interesting issue – though I have not personally heard of any case of the successful use of hypnosis to force someone to commit murder. Hypnosis is familiar in two main contexts: in entertainment and in medicine. With entertainment hypnosis, receptive subjects can find themselves being persuaded to do stupid things. From a Christian (and indeed common sense) perspective, allowing oneself to be such a subject is misguided, as we lose control of ourselves to some extent, and our personal and moral and indeed spiritual judgement is impaired. Christians engaged in deliverance ministry (freeing people from destructive spiritual captivity) have found people to be badly affected, spiritually, by such thought-control. Hypnosis is also used in medical and quasi-medical contexts.

But there is a context where people are persuaded to do things that in their saner moments they would consider criminal. This thought-control is not achieved by hypnosis or technological gadgetry, and it is this that we usually refer to as 'brainwashing'. Probably the most well-known case was that of Patty Hearst, daughter of the famous media magnate Randolph Hearst, who was captured by a far left quasi-religious cult termed the Symbionese Liberation Army. The 19-year-old student Hearst was kidnapped in 1974. Within three months, she was caught on security camera with a machine-gun, as a fully committed SLA member, taking part in a bank robbery. Eventually, after some SLA members were killed, Hearst was traced, but through her trial continued to profess her allegiance to the SLA. Meanwhile, her defence claimed she was brainwashed. She was convicted and sentenced to seven years, but released after two, following a pardon from President Carter.

The SLA was a weird cult with political aims and few members, but their ability to persuade their kidnap victim to believe in their cause to such an extent showed how successful brainwashing by a cult could be.

A more conventionally religious cult I came across personally back in my first year at Cambridge University 1972–73 was what we now call the Moonies, then working under the name 'The Unified Family', and which at that time had a big push to persuade students to enlist. The strategy advertised 'America for only £10?' – and told interested students they could have six weeks in America for £10, all travel and accommodation costs paid for. All they would have to do was 'help' in a 'holiday camp' for five weeks; the sixth week would be free for them to do what they liked, and their return journey paid for. It was a less cynical age, and many students took the opportunity of a free holiday, assuming the five weeks would mean helping children, or needy people. Few read the small print that made it clear that if they defaulted in attending the five-week course they would have to pay their own way home. And the five-week course turned out to be a five-week indoctrination course in the teachings of Sun Myung Moon. Our network of college Christian Unions had warned people strongly against the sect. However, some Christians and many others attended.

Some months afterwards, our student union newspaper carried a highly revealing article showing the effectiveness of the brainwashing. Once people had arrived and discovered to their horror that they faced five weeks more indoctrination, they faced a terrible dilemma: Should they try to stick it out for the five weeks, and hope to make it to the free week and free return, or should they default, knowing they were stranded? This was before credit cards and easy international phone calls, and so those students who defaulted were marooned.

According to the student article, those in this dilemma fell into three groups. There were those who feared they would not survive the five weeks, and defaulted. They had to solve their new problem, somehow finding the work that would enable them to raise the money to fund their fare home. There were those who successfully endured the five-week course, and came home 'sadder and wiser' after the event. And there were those who tried to endure the course, but ended up becoming Moonies, brainwashed by the incessant indoctrination.

What was the difference between those able to resist brainwashing and those who failed? According to the student who had witnessed this, there were basically two groups of students that managed to resist indoctrination: the committed Christians and the committed Marxists (this was 1973, and there were still quite a few of them). In other words, those who were able to resist brainwashing were those who had a strong belief in something already, those who had some reference-point which enabled them to stand up to this prolonged pressure.

In an age which has made a supposed virtue of not believing strongly in anything, but of being 'cool' and uncommitted, the result is that such people today are actually more vulnerable to brainwashing.

Of course, those who are already sympathetic to the aims of a cult will be much easier to indoctrinate. Ordinary moderate people who already have some sympathy for the aims of cults that use suicide bombing are going to be easier to enlist than those who reject their aims.

So the danger of Cybercontrol, or brainwashing, comes not through conventional hypnosis or technological forms of mind-control, but in a religious or quasi-religious context. And once again, *Doctor Who* has overlooked, or at least not fully recognised, the dangers of religion gone wrong – and still less spotted the benefits of religion gone right in resisting such brainwashing.

Discussions: This chapter raises the question of freedom. Does the Internet enhance true freedom?
This chapter argues that a person 'free' of strong beliefs is more vulnerable to persuasion by others, including odd groups and cults. What do you think gives a person strong, inner freedom?

Epilogue

Looking back, looking forward

There is little doubt in my mind that the resilience of the fan base of *Doctor Who* has kept it alive over the past two decades, despite all the attempts to bury it. And in the absence of *Doctor Who* on TV, there have been many other avenues for creation of *Doctor Who* over this period. Many fans of the series in the 1960s, lamenting the loss of the episodes junked by the BBC in the 1970s, have worked very creatively on a programme of increasingly enhanced reconstructions of the missing episodes, available through various websites. These use stills, audiotapes and surviving video clips. Many writers continued the stories of the Seventh Doctor, in the form of novels (*The New Adventures of Doctor Who*), introducing new companions, like the interesting archaeologist Bernice Summerfield. These have been augmented by the so-called *Missing Adventures*, which are similar novels, but set during the time of earlier Doctors and companions. Then there are the *Big Finish* audio series we have mentioned several times. And these new forms of *Doctor Who* continue to be made, alongside new *Doctor Who*. Indeed the Ninth Doctor (now already past!) is getting the same treatment of new novels.

But the TV series continued with *The Christmas Invasion* at the end of 2005, and a full raft of 13 episodes in season two in 2006 (and more to follow in 2007), including stories with returning villains of the new series, of the old series and, of course, Sarah Jane Smith, companion of the Third and Fourth Doctor, with K-9. They had their own unsuccessful spin-off in 1981. Captain Jack Harkness is due to get a full 13-episode spin-off exploiting his character after the watershed in a series to be called *Torchwood* (an anagram of *Doctor Who*). This is planned for late 2006. As for *Doctor Who* itself, the series will introduce new perils and old, and introduce us to new historical encounters as well. Queen Victoria was the focus off-stage with earlier Doctors (*Ghost Light*; *The Curse of Peladon*), but will be on-stage in season two.

But as we look back – and forwards – not just at the series, but at this book's reflections on it, and the implications of them, what have we seen?

Evil must be fought

Doctor Who is an adventure series, in which the Doctor faces down the problems of evil. We started with Autons and ended with the Cybermen. Right at the start, the Second Doctor reminded us that 'evil must be fought', and it was the Cybermen he had in mind.

Throughout this book, we have been reminded of many different forms of evil, and some forms of resistance to it. These evils have included many cases of those who, in order to make their race thrive, are quick to destroy others (or try to) if they think it to their advantage. Both the Nestene Consciousness and the Slitheen family were happy to destroy humanity for their own benefit. Evil also often includes deceit, as with the Slitheen, Cassandra, the Jagrafess and especially the Gelth (not to mention Adam). But a running theme is how we may become victims of our own technological success, developing medicine at the expense of morality and humanity (Cybermen), the ultimate weapon that might destroy its makers (Daleks), or the nanobot that mistakenly runs amok, destroying us by accident.

However, there are other tough choices, like Adam's sin, and Rose's recklessness, both potentially wrecking trust placed in them, and there are the challenges faced by Rose herself, and by Mickey, Jackie and Pete. Actually, most of the suffering that most people experience is not caused by megalomaniacs like Hitler, Saddam or bin Laden. The suffering they cause is headline news, and truly dreadful for those who face it. But most pain experienced by most people is caused by pretty ordinary people. And the positive counterpoint is that the most inspiring and encouraging experiences most people will have will be caused by ordinary people, too. So the challenges for ordinary people in *Doctor Who* bring the conflicts with evil and dangers much closer to home.

What we have also seen is not simply evil portrayed, or even evil simply defeated. We have seen a whole variety in the ways in which the Doctor resists evil; the old saying 'know your enemy' is often key – typically, while everyone else might want to flee, the Doctor will be heading in the opposite direction, to face the evil down and try to find out what his enemies are doing.

As we saw, the Doctor tried many different ways of resisting evil. These included: diplomacy; intelligent questioning; inspiring others to join him in the struggle; being prepared to sacrifice himself to save others; and, more controversially, killing the evil creatures to stop them killing. And we saw how the 'last Dalek' was defeated, not so much by superior weaponry, but by becoming humanised. Though this was accidental, it reminds us that often we make better progress by humanising rather than demonising our opponents.

The most frequent refrain from the forces of evil, in *Doctor Who* and much other SF, is 'resistance is useless'! But what we have seen is that resistance is not useless; it is essential.

Final thought: Since evil takes many forms, e.g. greed, megalomania, and weakness in the face of temptation, what should be the different ways we respond to the challenges we face?

What resources might help us?